SLAUGHTER AT BLUEWATER LAKE

Drawing pictures of hard cases on Wanted notices was a tedious task for Nick Paget. But when he was asked to draw one that fitted his own description, he resolved to ride back into the storm of trouble he thought he had left behind . . . The shores of Bluewater Lake were lashed with deceit, lies and lust for gold. Nick faced drowning in a quagmire of evil. Sudden death was all around him . . . Now, in a savage gun battle, with the innocent dying alongside the guilty, he must face his enemies gun to gun.

Books by Bill Morrison
in the Linford Western Library:

THE WOODEN GUN
A DOLLAR FROM THE STAGE
CHEYENNE NOON
RIVER GOLD
DESERT DUEL
REVENGE COMES LATE
BUSHWHACKER

BILL MORRISON

SLAUGHTER AT BLUEWATER LAKE

Complete and Unabridged

LINFORD
Leicester

First published in Great Britain in 2005 by
Robert Hale Limited
London

First Linford Edition
published 2006
by arrangement with
Robert Hale Limited
London

British Library CIP Data

Morrison, Bill, *1931* –
Slaughter at Bluewater Lake.—
Large print ed.—
Linford western library
1. Western stories
2. Large type books
I. Title
823.9′14 [F]

ISBN 1–84617–283–7

Published by
F. A. Thorpe (Publishing)
Anstey, Leicestershire

Set by Words & Graphics Ltd.
Anstey, Leicestershire
Printed and bound in Great Britain by
T. J. International Ltd., Padstow, Cornwall

This book is printed on acid-free paper

1

'Grey beard — that was it — he had a grey beard.'

'Like this?' Nick scribbled with his chalk on the board in front of him. 'This length, do ya reckon?'

'Nope, longer,' said the little fat man.

'Thet's about it,' disagreed the man in the checked shirt.

Nick shrugged. Beards grew by the day and were easily shortened. It did not matter. Witnesses always saw things differently even in important points of identification. Beards were usually easily enough controlled by men on the run from the law. He needed better than this if he were to make up an accurate sketch for a Wanted notice.

'What else?' he asked patiently.

'Green eyes,' said the little fat man.

'More like grey,' grunted the man in the checked shirt.

'Like mine?' asked Nick, curbing his irritation.

'Yeah, somethin' like yourn . . . '

'What else? Anything unusual that you can remember? What about the nose?'

'Big. Kind of hooked.'

'Aquiline?'

'Naw. Long and bent — like a vulture or somethin'.'

'Or an eagle, maybe . . . That was it — like an eagle's beak!'

'He has two teeth missin' at the front,' remembered the checked shirt.

'Yeah, thet's right!' agreed the fat one. 'Looked like somebody had slugged him with a pick-axe handle!'

Well, that was something to go on, thought Nick as he crayoned in the mouth under a large, bent nose and a straggling moustache. The bank robber couldn't change his teeth or his nose . . .

'What was he wearing? You remember anything?'

'Long coat. Dirty lookin'. Carried a

Colt too. Swore like hell all the time.'

It didn't seem that anything more was forthcoming from these two bystanders who had happened to be in the street just when the escaping bank robber had allowed his bandanna to slip from his face.

'All right,' said Nick with an air of finality. 'I got a couple of other people to see. Thanks for your help.'

'We get something for this, don't we — for comin' all this way and everything?'

'Sure, see the sheriff. He'll give you travelling expenses and a bit more.'

They went out of the doorway of the little room and turned into the sun-baked street towards the sheriff's office. Nick sighed. It was always hard to find agreement from witnesses. Folks were notoriously unobservant at times of high excitement or danger. He knew the ink drawings he made from his crayon sketches to be sent to the larger town of Parksville for printing and then for distribution over the territory were only approximations at best. It seldom happened that they were instrumental in bringing a criminal to justice.

Anyway, he was paid for it — not much but it helped to augment his modest income as clerk in the gunstore and paid for materials for his painting, which he hoped to make a career out of some day, although it was not easy to remain optimistic about that.

'Hey, Mr Munro, another feller for you to draw.' Alf from the sheriff's office had appeared in the doorway. 'Written description this time.' He grinned widely, showing tobacco-stained teeth. 'Sounds helluva lot like you! Ain't got a twin brother or anything? Same hair, same kind of face, about the same age.'

He shoved the paper on to the desk and ran off, still chuckling, while Nick lifted the paper and looked at it with a puzzled expression on his young features. What was this about a description that seemed to fit *himself*?

As he read the notice the faint smile went from his face and was replaced by amazement and then horror. Alf had been right about the resemblance. It could well have been a description of himself or a twin, if he had had one: fair hair, blue-grey eyes, high cheekbones, fair complexion, small ears — Jeeze! They had even got his ears right! — slight build — well, maybe years ago but not so slight now — twenty-two years old . . .

It was a description made by somebody who knew him well and had an eye for detail but all that paled into insignificance when he read the caption which went with it and which he was expected to print in large letters as the heading.

WANTED FOR MURDER.
NICK PAGET, FORMERLY OF
PRONGHORN FLATS,
MISSOURI . . .

Nick stood perfectly still in the pool of sunlight from the office window. The person who had given this description meant him! Every detail, even down to his age was accurate and the name too, for Paget had been his name until he left home years previously. His reasons for changing his name had been a puzzle to himself. He supposed it had just been to make a clean break with the past — that and to make sure that his father would not find out where he had gone . . .

But what could this mean — a wanted notice for himself — an accusation of murder made against him? He was entirely innocent of any crime — either at Pronghorn or anywhere else. None of this made any sense!

He sat down at the desk and read through the notice again, hardly able to believe his eyes, then he thrust the paper into a drawer as if to hide it from the world. For some minutes he stared blankly at the wall as his mind returned to his life at the farm near Pronghorn Flats. It had not been a happy one — at least after his mother had died when he was a small boy. He remembered his mother with affection, as she had always been a loving and caring person. His father had been very different — aloof, strict and harsh in his dealings with his young son.

After the death of his mother Nick's relationship with his father had worsened. There seemed to be no good reason for it. Nick had worked on the farm willingly enough and had attended to his schooling. His art work had earned him high praise from his teacher but none from his father. To Glen Paget drawing and painting were just a waste of time and he discouraged his son from indulging in them. Most of Nick's art was, therefore, done in secrecy whenever he had a few hours to spare on his own, usually when his father was away buying grain or livestock or visiting his brother, Robert, the lawyer, in Pronghorn.

Then, years after the death of Nick's mother, another woman had come to the Farm. Glen Paget had married again and to the amazement of the folks round about, she was young and pretty. Her name was Milly Anderson and she came from a tiny homestead about thirty miles away where the land had been overworked and most of the people found it hard to make a living. Folks in the vicinity of Pronghorn were puzzled as to why she had agreed to marry a man so much older than herself. Some reckoned she was motivated by the prosperous farm and the persistent rumours that Glen Paget was secretly a rich man; others believed she was not scheming at all but was just simple and fell for the pleasant grin and excessive flattery he could put on when he had a mind to.

Certainly, it was true that she often had a wandering, wayward look in her eye which seemed to suggest that her grasp on the realities of life might not be quite what they should have been.

In spite of all the doubt and secret criticism, it had happened, and Nick was pleasantly surprised to find his stepmother very easy to get along with. For one thing she was not many years older than himself, being only twenty-five at the time of her marriage, and she had a friendly and talkative personality, quite different from that of his old man. Also she was delighted to discover that Nick was a bit of an artist and gave him every encouragement to develop his talent.

The relationship was innocent enough, although Nick — if he had ever been honest with himself — would have had to admit that he found her attractive and could hardly think of her as his stepmother. He had a sneaking feeling also that she felt much the same about him and there were times when the knowledge that she was old Glen Paget's wife was hard to take.

Their friendship was doomed to come to nothing just the same, both being high-principled and brought up to respect the sanctity of marriage and family loyalty, in Nick's case, through the influence of his real mother rather than as a result of any teaching from his father, who — he had to admit — had been no more of a real father to him than the old Indian who helped with the horses.

Nevertheless, the friendly feelings between his young wife and his son by the previous marriage did not go unnoticed by old man Paget and he became increasingly jealous and suspicious, as was his nature. Nick saw it in the only half-concealed hostility in his father's eyes and sensed it in every word spoken. He tried as well as he could to avoid trouble but there seemed no way that his father could cease being suspicious of him. The explosion occurred one hot summer's afternoon when Glen Paget arrived back from Pronghorn Flats to find Nick attempting to make an oil-painting of Milly as she sat by the little flower-garden she had created since arriving at the farm.

Seeing his son and his young wife enjoying each other's company and watching them smile to one another as he arrived at the gate was the last straw for Glen Paget. With a shout of anger, his temper spilled over. He snatched the canvas from the easel and hurled it over the fence, into the grass and weeds of the nearby field. For a moment it seemed that he would strike his son, but then he glowered at his wife and told her to return to the house. Nick saw fear in Milly's face then and his heart sank as he realized the trap she had fallen into in this marriage.

Nothing was said between Milly and Nick thereafter. She went about her work in the house without looking at him, her face downcast, her eyes flitting to one side whenever she felt either of the men looking at her. All the time, Glen Paget looked morose with a deep fire of anger burning behind his eyes and a tension in his bearing that threatened to snap at any moment.

Nick realized then that he no longer had a place in the house and his continued presence would bring only disaster to Milly and danger to himself.

So it was that Nick left his home. He packed the few belongings he had and went into Pronghorn by mule-cart driven by one of the labourers. There he caught the stage travelling east for as far as his money would take him and had ended up in the small town of Deal.

Here he tried to rebuild his life and it seemed to him that he had succeeded pretty well in doing exactly that. This was the first time in over a year that he had thought seriously of his life at Pronghorn Flats. Now it had come back with a vengeance and in a way he could never have imagined.

He took the paper from the desk drawer once again and read it through, still almost unable to believe its contents. How could it be that he was accused of murder in Pronghorn when he had not seen the place in four years and had lived an honest and blameless life since?

There was no accounting for it. There was nothing at all in his memory that could have brought such an accusation against him even by mistake . . .

He pondered over the mystery for a long time. Then he thrust the paper back into the drawer and stood up with an air of decision. There was no way that he could remain where he was until the law caught up with him. He needed to go out to meet it and to clear his name in any way possible. He knew he could have gone round to see the sheriff of Deal to talk the matter out but he felt that would be a mistake. The sheriff would have had no option but to hold him in custody and Nick believed he had to be free to solve this mystery. As things were, no one in Deal suspected him of anything for the sheriff had obviously not connected the description brought in with yesterday's mail with the young feller who did the posters — and Alf's remark had been a mere joke.

A few minutes later he was back in the small room he rented above the grocery store and was packing his bag with a few items of clothing. Then he strapped on the gun he had bought from his employer a couple of years ago. It was a Colt 45, single-action army model. It had cost him a few months' salary to buy the revolver but he was confident in his ability to use it. He had learned to shoot as a young boy, shooting being one of the activities his father had approved of.

Then he caught the first stage heading in the general direction of Pronghorn Flats. Anxious to avoid questions, he said goodbye to no one and got on board as unobtrusively as possible, settling back in the seat to keep his head out of sight as the coach left town. There were only two other passengers on board, men from Parksville whom he did not know and who paid no attention to him except for the customary 'Howdy'.

He settled back in the corner with his hat over his eyes and pretended to sleep, although he knew sleep was impossible for him in his present state of turmoil. Suddenly it really hit hard into his mind that he was a wanted man. The idea made him feel like shouting out in protest but he curbed the impulse and remained still, his thoughts raging as he tried to figure out what could possibly have led to the present situation.

But there was nothing. He had never shot a gun in anger, let alone murdered anyone. There was simply no explanation he could come up with. All he could do, as he saw it, was to return to Pronghorn and find out what this was all about. Then he changed his mind about that. If he were to get off the stage in the main street of Pronghorn Flats he would be immediately recognized. He had not been away so long that everyone would have forgotten him. He might even find himself face to face with the sheriff. Who was the sheriff? It had been Clem Burns when he had left and likely enough still was. Not a man to be trifled with!

No, it would be a mistake to stay on the stage until it reached Pronghorn.

He must get off before then and travel the rest of the way on foot or on horseback — if he could somehow get a horse. He made up his mind to go straight home. He would walk into the farm in which he had been brought up and ask his old man what this was all about. There was no reason, surely, for the continued jealousy of Glen Paget after all this time!

The journey by stagecoach took the best part of three days and Nick was forced to spend two nights in cheap boarding-houses along the way. The accommodation was poor and the food just as bad but even so he saw his small amount of savings rapidly dwindle. Not that he was too concerned about that. All he cared about now was to reach the vicinity of Pronghorn. If he had no money left then he would just have to sustain himself on fresh air or — if old man Paget was in a better frame of mind — a hunk of bread and cheese or a plate of beans.

Nevertheless, being in a state of agitation, Nick changed his mind again and asked the stagecoach driver to let him out in what seemed the middle of nowhere. He grinned back at the man who looked as if he thought the young feller was a bit crazy. Nick knew well enough that he was still about twenty miles from the Paget place but he had remembered the Hestons who used to farm just a short distance from where he now was.

The Hestons had been friends of his in happier times when he was young. The family consisted of two brothers, both a few years older than himself, and their kid sister. As far as he knew their parents had died many years before and they had made a success of the farm on their own. He remembered them as fine people and he felt sure they would welcome him and tell him what this was all about.

He trudged about a couple of miles along a narrow track between wide expanses of grass which led away from the main stage trail, swinging his suitcase in one hand and frequently wiping the sweat from his brow with the other. Long before he saw any sign of the Heston farm he caught sight of a rider coming along the track towards him. Within a few minutes, he realized it was a girl riding a white pony. She wore a white shirt and dark waistcoat and rode astride the saddle as many younger women were now in the habit of doing in the West. Her dark hair drifted out from under her black hat. Even from the distance, Nick could see she was pretty.

She drew her pony to a halt when she was still about a hundred yards away and scrutinized him with the wariness that becomes second nature to those who live on the edge of wild country. After a moment or two, however, he saw a flash of white teeth as she smiled. She moved the pony forward a little but kept at some distance from him.

'Hey, if it ain't Nick Paget! You

turned into a carpet-bagger or something? What are you selling from that suitcase?'

He recognized her now as Jayne Heston, grown up and with a beauty and a confidence she had never had before. What she said sounded like a joke but there was doubt in her voice, a strong hint of suspicion which told him that she knew he was a wanted man.

'It's me, sure, Jayne,' he answered. 'I'm glad to see you. You've sure changed some and all for the better too!'

He felt that his attempt to sound light-hearted was falling a bit flat.

'Where have you been all this time, Nick?'

It was almost like an interrogation. Her tone seemed to suggest it. He felt hurt but grinned at her as if his conscience was clear — as it was — although he had been feeling more and more like a criminal on the run with every passing hour of the last three days.

'Out East. Been living in a place called Deal.'

'You went away sudden. Didn't say goodbye to anybody.'

She urged her pony forward until she was almost at arm's length.

'No. Things were not so good at home. I've been living all right for the past few years but now it's all changed again for the worse. That's why I came back.'

She looked at him quietly, waiting for him to say more. Her eyes seemed to search him. They held many questions that she seemed unable for the moment to express.

'I hope you don't mind,' he said, his voice faltering a little, 'but I'm on my way to see you and your brothers. I need to talk. I'm not sure that my old man is the best person to talk to right now . . .'

He broke off as she stared at him. Her expression was of surprise and horror. In a second, however, it had gone and she looked at him in calm silence, waiting for him to speak again.

'Thing is, Jayne, the law seems to think I am a criminal — a murderer in fact! There's no truth in it! I don't understand it!' He was aware that his voice was rising with a suggestion of panic that he had not felt before. 'You've heard about this, haven't you? Everybody around here must know about it but what is it I am supposed to have done? How could I have murdered anyone? I've been away for four years, for God's sake!'

She was still staring at him but her eyes had softened. He felt that she believed him in spite of all.

The truth was that she did believe him. His reference to his father as the last person he could talk to had convinced her. It was either the truth as Nick saw it or a very bad, evil-minded joke. She did not think he was capable of such a remark in the circumstances. Even if he had been guilty it would have made no sense to speak in such a way if he thought to have her friendship and help. In any case, she remembered Nick from the past and it did not seem to her that he had changed so very much.

The pony moved forward and she extended her hand to him. He took it gratefully. Her fingers were small and tender. He smiled up at her.

'Nick,' she said gently, 'it seems to me that you don't know what you have been accused of. Your father's dead. They say that you killed him.'

2

He did not move for some moments as her words sank in. She looked down at him from the saddle with an expression of pity in her dark eyes. It was as if she had seen into his soul and was aware of the truth she detected there.

'I'm sorry, Nick,' she said at last, her voice trembling a little. 'I can see that was a terrible shock for you. Maybe I could have said it in a different way but — '

'There wasn't any,' he interrupted. 'But how come, Jayne? How is it that anybody can think a thing like that?'

'I don't know exactly but the story going round is that you and your father quarrelled years ago and you came back to get your revenge. They say you rode into the Paget place some months ago and shot your — your father dead! I never believed it Nick! It just what they all say.'

'Who says? Who thinks they saw me do a thing like that, for God's sake?' His voice now carried the anguish he felt — the feeling that had been with him, deep down, ever since that day in the little office in Deal. '*Me* — *me* a murderer — and my own father! It's madness!'

Jayne was silent, as if she sought to summon up courage to tell him the rest, then she took a deep breath.

'They say it was your stepmother — Milly?' she said. She pronounced the name as if somehow it did not fit in with the idea of a stepmother. 'She says she saw it all and that lawyer uncle of yours, the one who owns the place over by Bluecoat Ridge, he saw you around the district at the time.'

'I've been out East! I've been living at a place called Deal! I ain't never been near here in four years!'

'I believe you, Nick, but nobody else

will. Sheriff Burns has sent a description of you all over. He even wants a picture of you made up for a Wanted notice!'

Nick was silent as the irony of the situation sank in. He fought down his sense of rising panic, looking at the dust-covered trail as he did so. He did not want her to see any trace of fear in his eyes. He had a firm grip on his nerves when next he looked at her.

'I wanted to see your brothers, Jayne. They were always good friends of mine.'

'They would turn you in,' she answered bluntly but kindly. 'They're sticklers for the law, as I am — except when my womanly good sense tells me different. But listen, Nick, you can't go walking to the Paget place in this sun. You must have been out East too long if you think you can. You stay here. Sit down and rest. I'll be back as soon as I can and I'll bring you a horse.'

She rode away without another word and he watched her disappear over a rise in the trail. It was then that he felt utterly lost. All around the dry grasslands spread for miles. The sun beat down upon him relentlessly. There was nowhere he could go without meeting folks who would think of him as a wanted man and a murderer. He sat down in the grass and covered his eyes with the brim of his hat, just as he had done on the stage, but now he had the strange feeling of wanting to crawl into its shade and never face the world.

Jayne came back after what seemed to him to be a very long time and brought a spare horse with her. The horse was old and carried an almost worn-out saddle.

'This is the best I could do,' she said, almost apologetically. 'If I had taken one of the better horses it would have been noticed and my brothers would have gone out to search for it straight away. As it is, I made it look as if some careless hand had left the paddock gate open and it had strayed. They're too busy to worry about it right now.

There's some food and water too. I know you're going to the Paget place, Nick. I would too, if I was in your boots. Take it easy. Don't use that gun.'

She looked at him with a deeply serious and almost sorrowful expression across her pretty features.

'I hope things turn out better in some way, Nick. Maybe, if you see the sheriff and can come up with an alibi — that might do it. All this must be some crazy mistake. Milly must be wrong. The thing is, I heard tell she's been queer lately. I haven't seen her in two years. Before that we met sometimes in Pronghorn. She used to go to church . . . I had better go, Nick. I'm real sorry about all of this!'

'Thanks for your help, Jayne,' he answered earnestly, his voice choking as if his throat was full of dust. 'I'll repay you in some way if I ever can!'

He watched her once again until she was out of sight. He had the same lost feeling as before, then he turned and looked at the horse. It was dirty grey in colour with sad eyes and he felt a pang of pity for it as he realized it was being dragged into his troubles instead of being left in peace in the paddock. Still, it looked well-enough rested and there was no other way of reaching the Paget place in a reasonable time.

It was strange that he thought of the farm that had been his home for most of his life as just the 'Paget place', almost as if he had never been there. His father's death also meant nothing to him. Any love he had ever had for Glen Paget had died many years ago, even before the day when his oil-painting had sailed over the fence and Milly had crumpled under the weight of the old man's fury.

With a sigh, he mounted up and urged the old horse to take the trail west. The animal soon proved that a slow walk and an occasional canter were as much as it could manage and he did not try to force it to do better. Nevertheless, he appreciated being once more in the saddle. He had ridden a lot as a youth and even when living in Deal he had sometimes been able to borrow the gunsmith's horse for an afternoon. He had never been able to afford a horse of his own. Riding made him feel better — somehow more in control of his own life — although he knew it was illusory.

The sun was overhead and the heat was still oppressive but the grey made steady progress. As he rode he saw far away to the north the granite outcrop of Indian Rock, which stood by the river. The black thoughts he had experienced on the stage returned with renewed force. The information supplied by Jayne set his mind into a greater turmoil than ever. He was accused of killing his own father and his step-mother was witness against him. So, too, was his uncle, that sharp and successful lawyer who had inherited the place at Bluecoat Ridge at the same time as Glen Paget had taken over the farm beside Bluewater. What could any of it mean? Who was this man who had gunned down old Glen Paget?

For some minutes he wondered if it could have been a man who just looked like him. Alf, back in Deal, had made a joke about a double. Was that a possibility? Could some stranger with a grudge against Glen Paget, or just a bloody minded attitude, have ridden into the farm and killed him in front of his wife? Could that man have borne such a close resemblance to Nick that Milly had believed it to be Glen's own son who had done the shooting?

He clung on to the idea for some time before reluctantly rejecting it. It seemed impossible — *too* much of a coincidence!

His mind was still busy wrestling with black thoughts when the old grey horse climbed a low ridge and the farm could be seen ahead in the distance. Nick drew in then, suddenly overcome with an emotion he had never expected. He had thought sometimes of the place during his time in Deal but to see it again struck into his heart. The four years that had passed seemed to stretch in one moment into a century and it was as if he was looking into the past, when he had often sat up on this ridge and viewed the distant farm building; the main house, small but well-built of stone, the outbuildings of timber, the two paddocks and the fields lying all around, and beyond all of that, the little lake of Bluewater, reflecting in its depths the late afternoon sky.

He sat there for some minutes feeling strangely reluctant to continue on his way down the long grassy slope. It was as if there was a door before him, which he was afraid to push against because he knew there could be no peace on the other side of it.

He took a grip on his nerves and urged the grey on. The narrow track had long since run out but the slope was not so steep as to make any danger for the animal and he allowed it to go at its own pace, which was slow and easy.

As he drew nearer he realized that this was not the farm as he remembered it; fields were under weeds, fences were in a state of disrepair, a gate hung off its hinges. He saw too that there were no animals except for the mule in one of the paddocks, standing silently in the sparse shade provided by the old elm which stretched its branches across the fence. There were no hands around the place. No work had been done for a long time. That much was evident.

He entered the main gate, which stood open so that he did not need to dismount. The house looked as it had always done except for moss on the roof and a pile of old wood against the wall. At first there seemed no sign of life but then he caught sight of the old Indian, Feather Dan, who had been there for as long as Nick could remember. He still wore a ragged pair of overalls and a battered hat which half-covered his grey head. He was standing about fifty yards away with a broom in his hands as if in the act of making some desultory attempt to sweet the debris-covered path.

Nick smiled and waved a hand, pleased to see someone, but the old Indian only stared as if he had seen a ghost before he vanished behind a corner of the barn. The smile went from Nick's face as it came home to him that old Dan too regarded him as a criminal, best avoided. He dismounted and tied the grey to a hitching post before advancing with some trepidation, to the front door of the farmhouse. He knocked but received no answer, knocked again, with the same result, and then lifted the latch. It was in his mind to call out Milly's name but it would not come to his lips. He had an uneasy feeling it would be to call out the name of the dead.

The little porch was shabby in a way he could not remember it as being and there was an old coat — a man's coat — still hanging, dust-covered, on a hook. The door to the parlour pushed open with ease, and he entered, subconsciously touching the butt of his side-gun as he did so.

Milly sat at the fireside, staring into the empty grate. She was sitting still in a way that reminded him of a corpse. Her crumpled blue dress hung down to the faded carpet and she had on her lap a ragged piece of knitting and one knitting-needle. The other needle lay on the hearth. He noticed with some shock that there was a little grey in her hair and lines to her face that had not been there at all when he last saw her.

She seemed not to have heard him come in and he spoke to her in a quiet voice, using her name, while anxiety and some sense of the need for caution rose within him.

She looked up with clouded eyes as if not properly awake and stared in his direction as if peering into the shadows at some strange figure.

'Milly,' he said again, 'It's Nick. It's good to see you.'

The remark was trite and he knew it for he felt no pleasure in seeing her as she was and such empty remarks seemed out of place in the circumstances.

Slowly a gleam of recognition began to show through the dullness of her eyes. She moved and the knitting fell to the floor. She made as if to rise but then sat down once again on the hard chair.

'Nick!' Her tone of pleasant surprise brought a surge of joy into his heart and he stepped towards her, feeling suddenly ashamed that his hand had been on his gun as he entered the room. He took her hands in his and bent down as if to kiss her but he did not. The changes in her features, seen now at close quarters, made him draw in his breath as he realized how she had aged in four years that seemed now to have stretched beyond measure.

'How are you?' he asked, aware of the futility of the question as everything in her appearance seemed to answer it. 'Are you well?'

It was like approaching a timid wild animal with meaningless words, spoken in a gentle tone because it was only the tone that made sense. He knew, though, that the time had not yet come when he could ask the questions that filled up his mind.

'I'm all right,' she replied. 'Why did you come back, Nick? I thought you were away for ever. You went away without saying goodbye. It was a bad time, wasn't it? It was all angry — angry and crazy. He was all crazy! He was . . . ' Her voice broke off and then returned almost as a whimper. 'He was mad. He was hitting! It was that time, wasn't it? But you went off. There was nobody here but me and him.'

The words brought a chill to Nick's heart and a flood of guilt. Jeeze, had it been as bad as that? If he had known, he would have stayed. He would not have left her. He should not have gone and left her to face it! If he had remained on the farm he could have done something. Only it had seemed the best move at the time. He had not guessed that Glen Paget was on the verge of anything like that! God curse him! Curse old man Paget — and himself too, for his stupidity!

He sat down on the little wooden chair opposite her and stretched out his hands to grip her own. Her hands were still soft, not worn hard by the work of the house and farm. Whatever else Glen Paget had made of her it had not been a drudge. Other things had been happening.

'My, I remember that picture you painted of me, Nick!' She smiled suddenly like a child reminded of a birthday. 'It was so nice! You painted me just as I was. You got all my prettiness!'

'Yeah, I remember.' He smiled. 'It was real pretty. Like you!' He stared at her with pity as he saw how her prettiness had faded. 'I caught the sunlight in your hair.'

'You look sad, Nick.'

Her mood had changed a little. It was as if a cloud was beginning to blot out the sun. She bit her lip and he saw that it was not for the first time as the side of her mouth was marked as if she had a habit of chewing her lips in her agitation.

Nothing was said for a few minutes. Nick did not want darkness to cloud this meeting but he had come to find out what had happened and why he had been condemned in the eyes of all the folks of the district and was sought now as a murderer over all the territory. He could sense a change in her that held foreboding. His mind sought ways of asking the huge question that hung like the shadow of the gallows across him but he was afraid. Something in her inner tension warned him to find the right words or to remain silent.

It was then that he heard a sound in the yard outside. He jumped up suddenly and moved to the grimy window just in time to see the old Indian, Feather Dan, unhitch the grey and lead it away towards the gate.

'Hey!' Nick yelled out and quickly rushed from the room, through the tiny porch and was outside in a moment. But he was too late for the Indian had mounted more quickly than seemed likely for an old man and had forced the horse into a gallop such as Nick had not imposed upon it.

Horse and rider were out through the gate within seconds. Nick drew his gun but did not fire. Shooting a man in the back, especially a man whom he had at one time counted as a friend, was not in his nature. He knew for certain where Feather Dan was heading. The Indian was riding as fast as he could into Pronghorn to warn the sheriff that the murderer had returned. Nevertheless, it would be a mistake to kill the fleeing man because then he really would be a murderer.

Nick hesitated, hand still on his Colt, and in that few seconds Feather Dan screamed and fell from the grey as a rifle boomed no more than a yard from Nick's shoulder.

Nick swung round in amazement to see Milly beside him, the smoking

Winchester still raised, her face twisted in a mixture of rage and panic as she peered along the sight.

For a moment Nick stood thunderstruck. He could not believe what he was witnessing. Never in all the time he had known Milly would he have thought she could fire a shot at another human being, and one evidently intended to kill.

The Winchester was lowered, muzzle to the ground. Milly stared out through the gate to where the prone form of the Indian lay in the dirt. The man did not move. A little way beyond, the grey had come to a halt, showing no sign of fear but a little relieved to find itself without the weight of the rider and in no need to gallop.

Milly was sobbing. The rifle fell from her hands. She looked at Nick with an expression of wild appeal.

'He was . . . going for Sheriff Burns! He was going to tell. I know it!'

'I know,' replied Nick, 'but — '

'I had to do it! They would come and

take you away and hang you!'

'Yeah, but I guess they'll come anyway. It needs to be faced up to sometime. Look here, Milly, I'll go see to Dan. Maybe it's not too late.'

He ran from her and within a moment had turned Feather Dan over on his back so that his face could be seen. The Indian was still alive. There was blood staining his overalls. He was unconscious from the fall but his breathing seemed about normal. Nick drew the slack overalls and dirty shirt aside until he could see the injury. There was a nasty wound in his shoulder that bled profusely but was not likely to be fatal. Nick straightened himself up and looked back towards the house, intending to ask Milly for water and some kind of a bandage so that the wound could be attended to before the man was moved.

She was not there. The door still stood ajar. She had gone back into the house with her rifle as if she had no further interest in Feather Dan or what she had done to him.

Nick strode quickly to the door and walked in without ceremony. The need to try to do something for the wounded man was paramount in his mind. She was standing by the window on the other side of the room from the one facing the yard. It looked on to a little garden, long since gone over to weeds but colourful in its display of wild flowers. The rifle butt rested on the floor. She held the muzzle a few inches under her chin.

'Milly,' he said, trying to control the agitation in his voice, 'Feather Dan needs to be helped.'

Milly swung round. The Winchester rose and pointed straight at him. The barrel did not waver.

'You killed him! You killed Dan! Just like you killed Glen! I remember all of it! You came riding in here that day and shot Glen like as if he was a mad dog! That was my husband you killed, you murdering snake! You did it for your own revenge because he drove you off for trying to mess about with me! They'll hang you and it will be right that they should. He was a good . . . a good husband. Any wife would be proud of him . . . '

Her eyes were wild. For a second he was reminded of a lynx he had come face to face with in the woods when he was a boy. It had scared him. Milly's eyes drove into his soul for they held the light of madness and the fear and anger of the damned.

'Milly, it ain't true. None of that is right! I've not been here in years.'

For a moment she did not answer him. The rifle remained steady. When she spoke it was in a hiss scarcely recognizable as human.

'I could shoot you down like you shot Glen but it will be better to see you hang. The gallows will bring your death. The gallows . . . the gallows . . . ' Her features twisted further as a wild fear came into her. 'The gallows will be a terrible death . . . terrible . . . ' She sobbed and the rifle shook before she pointed it straight at him again. 'They will take you to it. Not me . . . not me . . . '

3

Feather Dan slowly regained consciousness. At first he had no idea where he was or what had happened. The darkening sky seemed like a blanket that hung over him, clogging up his mind and suffocating his memory. By slow degrees only did he piece together the events that took place before darkness fell upon him. He remembered leading away the grey horse and climbing into the saddle, then the noise of the shot and the violent blow which accompanied it. He caught a sudden vision in his mind of the young feller, Nick, and the memory made him attempt to sit up because he knew then what he had to do.

Pain swamped through his body. His shoulder and arm screamed out at him, begging not to be moved. He lay still, strangely astonished at his helplessness, and then with a supreme effort, twisted himself round, put his left hand on to the earth and tried to rise. He became suddenly aware of blood flowing through his shirt and dribbling into the dirt. He attempted to kneel but collapsed on to his face.

He looked up, eyes almost level with the ground, and saw the old grey horse standing some yards away. It was looking at him with sad eyes as if it pitied him for his pain and weakness. He felt he had to reach it so that it could carry him to Mr Paget. Taking a deep breath, he gritted his teeth against the agony of his wound and dragged himself like a dying crab towards the horse but it moved slowly backwards and then turned to trot off as if its new found freedom was too fine a thing to be given up easily.

Dan fell back. He knew he had been hit by a rifle bullet and not by a shot from a handgun. He had recognized the distinctive boom and recalled who had pulled the trigger. The knowledge pained him but did not bring anger as he knew it was the wild spirits in her head that had caused it to happen.

Nevertheless, he must get back to Mr Paget to tell him that the young feller had come back because it was the only way in which all this terrible mess could be cleared up and peace come to replace the trouble that had been everywhere around for so long. He tried again to push himself upright but now his head and shoulders and arms seemed to have turned to stone and he could not move.

Some short distance away in the farmhouse Nick stood quite still as the muzzle of the rifle still pointed at his stomach. The eyes behind it were still wild and her trigger-finger shook. For a few seconds which seemed like an eternity no word passed between them. When she eventually spoke the tone of her voice had fallen to a low and frightening level.

'You killed Dan! You'll hang for it,' she repeated. 'I'll take you to the sheriff. He'll know what to do with you.'

Nick was looking at her with the concentration of a man suddenly confronted by a dangerous animal. He saw the light change in her eyes a little. There came a hint of doubt — a flicker of uncertainty.

'Milly,' he said quietly, 'nobody has been killed.'

'You fired at him!'

'Nobody on this farm killed him and no one knows who fired the gun,' he lied. 'The thing is, Milly, he's still alive but he needs help. We can save him and then nobody will have been killed. Nobody will be to blame. Let's save Feather Dan, Milly! We can do it and then everything will be all right!'

He watched closely, knowing that any word he had said might have brought about some little twist in her distraught mind that could finish him. Then came a tiny light shining through the mist of insanity. Her countenance brightened. A smile hovered round her lips.

Suddenly, as if she held nothing more dangerous than a ladle in her hands, she placed the Winchester on the table and turned for the door.

'I'll get water,' she shrilled in a sudden determination to help the wounded man. 'I'll get a basin from the kitchen!'

Nick did not move for a moment. He knew that death had passed by him and he had felt it stroke his shoulder. His hands trembled but then he got a grip on his nerves.

'What about bandages?' he asked. 'Is there anything we can use?'

'There's some linen in the drawer in the other room,' she called back to him as if common sense and charity had never deserted her. 'We must hurry! He needs all our help!'

Nick hurried into the next room and found the piece of linen in the drawer as she had said. He pulled it out and began to cut it into strips with his knife. There was nothing else but a few pieces of cloth in the drawer and as he looked round the room he suddenly realized that there was nothing much else in the room either. He had a sudden vision of his surroundings as they had been in the past. There had been pictures, glass vases, a pair of china peacocks, a willow pattern dinner-set, two silver candle-sticks and a bronze bust of General Sherman. It had all gone. The furniture was bare but for a layer of dust. He realized that the other room was no better. Everything of value or attractive in itself had been taken away.

Milly was running out through the door with a basin in her hands. He ran after her, carrying the strips of cotton, his mind in turmoil, wondering what had happened in these four years — beginning to wonder too as to his own state of mind.

Feather Dan had fallen into unconsciousness. Milly cleaned the wound with a suddenly expert hand while her face displayed deep anxiety. Nick found to his relief that the bullet had gone right through the flesh so that there would be no question of attempting the harrowing business of digging it out with a knife. That would have demanded the attentions of a doctor and he knew he did not want to bring in a doctor right now. There were questions to be answered before then.

Nick placed his hands under the old Indian's shoulders while Milly lifted his feet. Between them they carried him to the hut in which he had slept for many years. There was an old bed there with a dirty mattress and two dirty blankets. Nick glanced at Milly in surprise and disgust but did not show his feelings. It was too dangerous to do so. She seemed unaware of the dirt and helped to put Feather Dan into his bed with as much care as a nurse in a well-kept hospital. She fussed over him, checking his bandages and covering him carefully with the blankets.

Nick stood at the door of the hut, watching her, wondering how he could keep her in a balanced state of mind.

'I'll make Dan some coffee,' she said

brightly. 'That'll help him!'

'Sure, but only when he comes to,' put in Nick. 'He'll have to be properly awake or he'll choke.'

'I know, I know!' she snapped. 'But I'll bathe his brow first with cool water.'

She did so as Nick looked on. He was afraid to leave her, not knowing what she might do next. At last, Feather Dan began to breathe more easily and Milly decided to return to the house to put on the coffee. She seemed much more settled now and went about the task with quiet efficiency. When she went out with the mug of coffee, Nick took a chance and stayed indoors so that he could unload the Winchester of the two cartridges it still contained. He put the weapon on top of the tall dresser where she could not reach it without standing on a chair.

Milly came back smiling and saying that Feather Dan seemed better. Nick nodded as if he believed her and went out to see for himself. The Indian was lying still with his eyes closed but seemed to be breathing easily. Nick then went along the little stretch of trail leading from the gate and found the grey horse munching grass and weeds at the wayside. He brought it in and released it in the paddock. He was thankful when he found some hay in the barn and was able to feed it — and the mule, as it decided to join in.

When he went back into the house he found Milly slumped on the floor as if she had fallen asleep through sheer exhaustion. He raised her, helped her through to her bedroom and let her collapse on the bed which was untidy but much cleaner than that of old Dan.

He fell asleep in the parlour but awoke in the dim light of early dawn and went out with a candle to check on Dan's condition. The Indian was still asleep and looked in better shape. The wound had ceased to bleed and Nick felt that there was less need to worry. He went back inside and dropped asleep once more. He awoke with the sun shining into his face through the window. He stood up at once, not knowing what to expect on this day, and went into the kitchen where Milly was making coffee. She greeted him cheerfully enough and prepared a simple breakfast of eggs and buttered bread. He noted that there was a small supply of food in the cupboard but was certain that Milly had not left the farm to purchase it. It had come from the store in Pronghorn and he guessed that Feather Dan made one or two trips a week into town for the purpose. There was no work and no earning taking place on this farm but there was enough money to pay for meagre supplies.

He wondered about that but did not ask. She was looking at him across the table as he ate with some hint of puzzlement in her face, as if she was not certain what he was doing in the place at all but was too polite to question him.

'How's Dan,' he asked after a few minutes. 'He all right this morning?'

She stared in surprise.

'Dan? He's outside, I guess. He always gets to work early.'

Nick said nothing in reply but slipped out as soon as he had sipped a little more coffee and looked into the hut where he found Dan still lying with eyes closed but moaning a little and twisting his body in pain. Nick checked the dressing and found it still in place.

'Dan,' he asked quietly, 'how do you feel? Pain pretty bad?'

The eyes opened. Feather Dan attempted to grin but managed only a flicker of movement in his lips.

'All right . . . but what about Miss Milly? What about her?'

'OK just now, Dan. What's all this about? Why is everything so queer? Do you really think I killed my own father?'

Dan closed his eyes. He gave no answer. Then Milly appeared with coffee in a tin mug and a slice of bread mixed with milk in a bowl. The milk was sour but she did not notice it.

'Here, Dan,' she said kindly. 'Sup

this. It'll do you good.'

A little later Milly and Nick were back in the parlour and he looked up to check that the Winchester was still out of her reach on top of the dresser. It was still there, apparently unnoticed, but something else caught his eye. There was an old rectangular mark on the wallpaper. Suddenly he remembered the glass case containing the huge salmon that had hung there on display all his young life. The story had been that his grandfather had caught it in the falls when he came back from the Mexican war — God knows how many years ago. It had always been a valued family heirloom. Before he could restrain himself he had blurted out:

'The salmon, Milly, what the hell happened to the salmon?'

She stared at the place on the wall and then laughed.

'Back in the lake! That's where it is! It's back swimming in the lake where it should be!'

She laughed louder, seeming to think

her joke immensely funny. There was a hint of instability in her laughter and he resolved to ask her no more about it but she went on explaining and laughing in a voice that became more and more infected by hysteria.

'I threw it into the lake! Maybe it swam off! I threw in all the other things as well . . . the vases, the lousy pictures, the stupid bust of that buckaroo soldier he so much admired, the china peacocks, the willow pattern dinner-set, all his snakes and eagles . . . Ha, ha, ha . . . The goddamned sabre that his granddad used in some lousy battle, the brass lamp, the clock from the kitchen, his bed linen, the pots and pans, the knives and forks, his best riding-boots, his best coat! All of it went! I loaded it all up on the mule-cart and took it to the lake and unhitched the mule and let the whole godamned lot run down the bank and into the water! It sank like a stone except for a couple of his coats that floated away. The cart went down too at first, then it came up on its side with one wheel uppermost but it was empty. All the heavy stuff had gone down to the bottom into the very deepest part of the lake!

'Feather Dan helped me do it although he didn't really want to. He said it was a big mistake. Thing is . . . ' She glanced at Nick with a sly expression. 'Old Dan is just a beat-up old Indian who never did anything in his whole life except work around farms, but he worships me. Always has done since I came here. Thing is, he's in love with me and will do anything I ask him. He's just a kind of old burro really. Always does what he's told.'

Her words implied contempt for the old man but her tone was kindly. Nick stared at her and then said in a low, gentle voice designed not to alarm her in any way, a question that he could not contain:

'Milly, you say you just threw everything into Bluewater? Why? What did it mean?'

'It meant to hell with him!' There was

sudden anger in her voice now and he immediately regretted having asked her. 'He was evil to me! He did things to me that I didn't like! He didn't really love me. He spoke to me like as if I was a dog. All that stuff I threw away was his — or used to belong to that first wife of his — so it served him right! It was a way of getting back at him.'

She laughed shrilly, then her face changed to an expression of dismay. She looked mournfully at the floor and then wildly around the room almost as if she sought some way of escape.

'Then he came back. He was in town but he came back. He got angry! He was like a monster! He hit me! He knocked me to the ground — out there beside the paddock. He made my face bleed! It was like as if the world was all blowing up! He was roaring like a bear . . . it was like as if he was going to kill me . . . ' She ceased raving for a moment and sat perfectly still except for her hands shaking on the table-top. It was as if a vivid picture had come into her mind. She shuddered and struck her forehead with the palm of her hand. Suddenly she looked at Nick as if realization had dawned. 'Then you came riding in and killed him with your gun.'

'Milly! That ain't right! I wasn't even here!'

He could not contain his protest, although he recognized the danger of it.

She stared at him as though he had struck her, then terrible fear came into her eyes.

'No, no, it wasn't me! I never killed him! I won't go to the gallows . . . ' She shuddered as if in a fit, half-rose from her seat and thumped the wooden table with her fist. 'No, I will not! They won't hang me! You did it! Ask Feather Dan! Ask Robert Paget! He saw you around the place that very day. He told the sheriff about you. He's a lawyer! Don't you ever try to blame me for what you did!'

Nick fell silent as the truth came to him in a way that could not be denied.

He had suspected it but now it was clear. Milly had killed Glen Paget. She had done it because he was beating her and she had believed she might die.

She was afraid. She was in terror of the consequences of what she had done. The gallows loomed over her and she would do anything in the world rather than stand in its shadow. She was willing to send him in her place.

The knowledge hurt him like a stab wound to the heart. He had never been in love with Milly but he had counted on her friendship and had felt it to exist even when he was in far-off Deal. Now he knew she would push him ahead into death rather than face it herself.

Well, maybe it was not to be wondered at. She was weak, perhaps cowardly, and to be hanged was a fearful way to die. Many a man would feel the same as she did. There was little doubt that men had stood and watched as others died for crimes they themselves had committed. It was easy to boast — easy to swear that you yourself would not shrink from death if, by stepping forward into its shadow, you could save an innocent man — but in that last moment, it could not be a simple matter and the desire and the need to live would be likely to prevail.

So, the finger of accusation had been pointed at himself. Even so, he could not understand why. Would it not have been just as easy to invent a wandering stranger who had arrived at the lonely farm and gunned down Glen Paget? On the other hand, maybe Milly had blamed Nick simply because his was the first name to come into her head. She must have been questioned by Sheriff Burns and would very likely have said anything to divert suspicion from herself. As for Feather Dan, he would say anything she asked him to say, if it was a way of saving her from death.

Robert Paget, however, did not fit into the picture quite so easily. Why would this small town lawyer, prosperous enough with a good practice and a successful farm, tell such a lie about his own nephew? He had never cared in the slightest for Nick — a feeling that was mutual — but why help to condemn Nick in the eyes of the law by giving such misinformation?

It was not possible to believe that Robert Paget could think he had seen Nick at the time of the murder. He was not hovering on the verge of insanity like Milly nor was he an ignorant and easily led man like Feather Dan. Also, he had known Nick since birth and could not make such a mistake.

Why, then, had he made such a claim?

Milly was still shivering and casting agitated glances round the room as if expecting goblins to jump out at her. Nick, in spite of her accusation and his own looming danger, felt overcome by pity for her.

'Milly,' he whispered, 'it's all right. Nothing will happen to you. You didn't do anything. Take it easy.'

She seemed to calm a little as she

listened to his voice. When he rose to his feet he had decided what he must do. He could not accuse her of the crime he knew she had committed because there could be no justice resulting from it, even if he were to be believed which was highly unlikely. What right could there be in Milly going to the gallows for killing a man like Glen Paget who had treated her so badly that she had ended up hating him and, no doubt, going for a gun after or during the beating she had received? Sure, it was murder in the eyes of the law but the law did not see the human weakness and failure behind it all. It could not understand her state of mind. Even if it did and spared her the rope, it was certain that she would be sent back East to a grim institution where she would die slowly in misery. To Nick's way of thinking, that was even worse than the gallows.

To put her into the unfeeling hands of the law was not to be contemplated. Equally, he himself could not give himself up to suffer punishment for a crime he had not committed. As Nick saw it, there was nothing more to be done than to leave Bluewater for ever and become the wanted man he was already seen as being.

He went out to the shed where Dan lay. The Indian was conscious but in pain. He needed help and there was no way of fetching it unless Nick himself rode into Pronghorn or found someone who would pass on a message to the doctor in the town. There was a chance he could get someone to do that. If not, then he must ride to the doctor's house himself and then away like the wind before he could be detained by the law. But how could he make an escape on the old grey? Well, he would have to steal a faster mount. Might as well be hanged as a horse-thief as well as a murderer.

'Dan,' he said quietly, 'I'm going to ride into Pronghom to get help for you and for Milly. It'll be a risk but it needs to be done. I want you to get her to think that wound you have was the result of an accident. Tell the law that too. S'Long!'

He turned and went to the paddock where he caught the grey horse and saddled up. As he rode out through the gate he thought about Dan's wound and how unlike an accident it looked. The bullet had come from behind and from some little distance. It was hard for anybody to argue that the old Indian had clumsily dropped the rifle and shot himself. But maybe no one would examine the wound with the eye of a lawman. If they did then the blame would be levelled at Nick Paget who had returned for some strange reason and then had ridden away into the unknown.

4

Robert Paget stood just outside the doorway of his house on the farm at Bluecoat Ridge. It was a fine morning but he was not looking forward to spending the day in his office in Pronghorn Flats. There was legal work to do but it was routine and not well enough paid in his opinion. Also there had not been very much of it lately which brought a worrying aspect to it as he could see that his future as a lawyer in the small town might not be of long duration. That would be a matter of great regret to him as he had, when a young man, worked uncommonly hard to qualify and it was unpleasant now to realize that it might all come to an end in the middle years of his life without his achieving the success he had hoped for.

He might perhaps move to a bigger

town back East but that would mean leaving his farm, which had always done well enough. It was not very large, no bigger than his brother's place over at Bluewater and would never earn him the fortune he had always craved, but it was a livelihood and not to be given up without much consideration.

He was a man of portly build with thinning dark hair, only slightly grey at the temples, and a flabby face partly concealed by a drooping moustache. As always, when going into his office he wore a dark suit with a white shirt and cravat. In this respect, as in most others, he differed from his brother, Glen, who had never been known to wear a suit and had cared nothing for his appearance except during the time he had been courting Milly Anderson.

All that was, of course, now over, reflected Robert as he made ready to ride into town. His brother was dead and his sister-in-law, Milly, was still there, but for how long? Robert shook his head, a thin smile of amusement mixed with irritation spreading under his moustache, as his mind turned to the question of what was to become of Milly in the near future.

He had his own plans in that regard.

The lad who helped with the horses brought out the thoroughbred black called Midnight. It was a fine horse, the best Robert had ever seen. He looked at it admiringly and wished it was his own. Legally it belonged to Milly although Robert meant to have it for himself. That time had not yet come. After the tragedy over at Bluewater he had offered to help the distraught widow in every way possible and looking after her fine horse had been part of that offer. Her other horses and the rest of her stock of dairy cattle had been sold off as it was evident that she was not in a fit state to care for them, far less make them a commercial success.

Robert had looked after that part of the business and had given her the money from those sales so that she could continue to live as normally as possible with her servant, Feather Dan, after the remainder of the farm workers had been paid off. There was no use at all in her trying to run the place, as Robert had emphasized to everyone interested, as her state of mind would not allow it. A few folks had suggested that her farm might be sold but Robert had opposed the idea because he secretly wanted it for himself but had no intentions of paying for it and, in any case, lacked the funds to offer what folks would consider to be a fair price.

He rode towards town, checking as he went that his own workers were busy in his fields, then put his heels to the black and smiled in pleasure as it burst into willing movement. It was a splendid horse! He had first seen it four years ago when his brother had bought it as a yearling. It had come as a great surprise when Glen had bought such an expensive animal. There had been an even greater surprise not long afterwards when Robert had discovered that his brother had been in Pronghorn discussing the possibility of buying a pony and trap. Glen had never been one to consider such expensive luxuries. About the same time, it had come to Robert's ears that his brother had been discussing cattle with Jed Brandt, a cattleman who sometimes came through Pronghorn.

Robert knew Brandt as a dealer and range-owner who had been accused in the past of rustling, though the charge had never been proved or brought to court. He was suspected also of consorting with outlaws, although there had never been clear evidence of this either. Robert had never discounted the likelihood, however, but — lawyer though he was — he did not find the idea in anyway reprehensible, as some of his own dealings in the past could not have withstood the light of day. He had made a point of making the acquaintance of Brandt, in order to find out more about the proposed deal. Brandt had let it be known that Glen's interest had seemed to be that of a man who was thinking about going into cattle as a business venture, and had even been talking about buying several hundred head as a start.

All these indications of his brother's prosperity had come as a great shock to Robert, although only the purchase of the thoroughbred had actually been accomplished. The pony and trap and the cattle deal had only been in the negotiation stages when Glen had met with his untimely end. But it set Robert thinking hard and his mind had turned to where it had often been before throughout his life, which was back to his father, old man Busby Paget, who had gone off to the Mexican war as a freckle-face youth with scarcely a cent in his pockets and had come back as a rich man.

So it was rumoured. There must have been truth in it too because he bought Bluewater farm as soon as he got back and not very long afterwards had set up the place at Bluecoat Ridge. Land was cheap then, certainly, but two well-stocked farms with fine houses could not have been created out of nothing.

And there was the question of the mule train . . .

'Hey, Mr Paget!' The youthful voice aroused Robert from his reverie and he looked round sharply to see a boy of about thirteen waving at him from the long grass. 'I've seen Nick — you know — your nephew! You asked me to tell you if I ever saw him!'

Robert gasped and drew rein.

'You sure about that, Jasper?' It seemed unbelievable. Although he had asked this lad and others to let him know if they ever saw Nick, he had not really expected that they ever would.

'Sure thing, Mr Paget. I saw him from the top of the ridge. He seemed to be coming from Bluewater an' goin' to Pronghorn. Riding a grey horse. Goin' pretty slow like as if he's keeping his eyes peeled.'

Robert stared hard at the lad but could not but believe him. Jasper was smart with sharp eyes and he knew Nick Paget from former years. If it were true then there was no time to lose. He had better get into town to warn the sheriff with all speed.

'Good boy, Jasper!' He threw the lad the first coin his fingers touched from his pocket and set his heels to the black. It broke into a gallop along the dusty trail while Robert's mind also worked at breakneck speed. What had Nick been doing at Bluewater Farm? Why was he now heading towards Pronghorn? Could the black make town before Nick did so that Sheriff Burns could be warned in time? Would Nick ride into town at all or did he have some other errand which took him only in that direction with the result that he would soon turn tail and ride swiftly on his way out of danger?

The distance from Bluecoat Ridge to Pronghorn was a little shorter than that from Bluewater and the thoroughbred could be relied upon to outpace most horses. The chances were Robert would get there first. The thought of Nick being taken into custody pleased Robert mightily. All his plans would work out even more quickly than he had hoped. Nick being committed for murder of his own father, would suffer the consequences and would be out of the way for ever. That would leave only Milly to inherit Glen Paget's land and his money. Her state of mind would very soon put her into an institution for the insane and everything would then go to Glen's brother, Robert.

If Milly, in spite of all Robert's planning and persuasion of certain parties, remained at Bluewater, then a woman in her mental state could easily fall victim to an accident and that would be the whole matter settled.

So all the land would come into Robert's hands. More important, as he saw it, was the question of the Mexican silver. Old man Busby had brought mules laden with silver back from the Mexican war. It was reputed to be in coin, although neither Glen nor himself had ever seen any of it. How much there had been was a matter of much conjecture. Some old people had said there were two mules, others reckoned there had been about six or eight. The mules had been dead for decades and no one alive had ever seen the silver. Privately, Robert believed that Busby had hidden his loot over at Bluewater or very close to the place. He was equally convinced that Glen had discovered it a few years ago and that had turned him from a careful farmer, who had to watch every cent, into a potential cattleman, thinking of owning hundreds of head of beef, and looking to buy a pony and trap for his own pleasure.

Strong though the black was, the ride into Pronghorn Flats that morning was a test of its endurance and it was blowing hard and frothing at the mouth by the time Robert came in sight of the main street. Robert kept it going until he arrived at the sheriff's office and there he dismounted as rapidly as his portly body would allow. He wasted no time in entering the office where he found Sheriff Burns and his deputy, Lamprey, standing at the desk studying the daily newspaper.

They both looked round in surprise at his sudden arrival. Burns was about fifty years old, grey and lean, but a hard man, well able to control the minor troubles with drunks and occasional rowdy cowmen who came through Pronghorn. He was also quite capable of dealing with more serious matters, as two outlaws now lying in the town graveyard could have testified had they been capable of finding the words. Lamprey, tall and sparsely built, was quick with a rifle and had a reputation as a sharpshooter.

'Sheriff,' gasped Robert, 'Nick Paget has turned up. He's riding down the trail from Bluewater. Now's the time to get him!'

Burns stared. He was surprised at the news but never failed to be surprised also by Robert Paget, who for the last few months had lent every encouragement to the law in its efforts to achieve the arrest of his own nephew. It was, of course, understandable, the murder victim being his own brother, but there was an eagerness about Robert that had never seemed quite to fit with his position of uncle to the suspect.

'You're sure, Mr Paget?' asked Burns. 'You seen him yourself?'

'That kid, Jasper, saw him,' explained Robert. 'He's a reliable boy and good with his eyes. I'll wager he hasn't made a mistake.'

Burns considered only for a moment. It was a possible sighting of the criminal and not one to be ignored. He had believed Nick Paget to be far away, probably back East, but maybe he had returned for some reason of his own.

'All right, Joe,' he said to Lamprey, 'get some of the men together and we'll ride out right now.'

The posse was not long in forming and seven riders, including Robert, were soon on their way up the trail leading to Bluewater. The route led through undulating country so that it was not possible to see very far ahead. Burns did not want to come across the outlaw unexpectedly, as he wanted to avoid shooting.

'Midge,' he said, 'tell you what. Ride up ahead and if you sees this feller, turn around — real casual like — and come back to tell me. Look as if you are jest riding along with nothin' on your mind . . . and, Mr Paget, you should hang back aways. You ain't really part of this posse. I appreciate how you feel, it being your relatives and all, but keep well back. No point in your gittin' shot when it gets rough.'

Midge was a small man who had recently come to the region and had shown from the start that he wanted to be a deputy. Burns had liked his style and had enrolled him in that capacity. He was also a stranger to Nick Paget and therefore less likely to arouse suspicion when he was seen by the suspect.

The little man was only too happy to oblige. He was always keen to prove himself as a lawman and grinned as he spurred his horse into the vanguard. Before long, he saw Nick approaching about quarter of a mile up the trail. Midge recognized him easily, having been made familiar with the young man's appearance from repeated descriptions. He did not turn back, as instructed, but rode forward, waving a hand in friendly greeting.

'Howdy!' he called as Nick drew nearer. 'I'm lookin' for Bluecoat Ridge. You know its whereabouts, sir?'

Nick was not entirely on his guard. He had been riding towards Pronghorn, intending if necessary, to enter the town, but hoping to meet someone whom he could entrust with a message to the local doctor. If so, he would pull out and head for distant parts. He was a little relieved to see this stranger, who seemed friendly.

'Well, thing is — ' The words were not out of his mouth when Midge drew level and had produced a pistol which he pointed at Nick's stomach.

'Reach fer the sky,' grinned Midge. His free hand was gripping the head harness of the grey; the hand holding the gun did not waver. 'Move and you're a dead man, Paget!'

The two men remained where they were. Nick, dismay written all over his face, held his hands in the air. Midge, both hands occupied, did not attempt to take his prisoner's gun as the movement could change the situation for the worse. As things were, he was well satisfied. He had settled the affair with no help from the rest of the posse and needed only to wait a few minutes until they appeared over the rise in the trail. He reckoned he had proved himself as a smart lawman.

Burns scowled at having his orders ignored but was happy that there had been no shooting. He disarmed Nick and bound his hands behind his back. Nick felt like falling from the saddle in his despair but said nothing and made every effort not to appear afraid.

'Well, well,' said Burns gruffly, 'I'm sure glad to take you in so easy but reckon it's a mortal shame that it was ever necessary. You seemed a decent enough feller when you were young. I never thought to see you finish up this way!'

It was true. Nick remembered Burns as a kindly man who always had a friendly word for him in former times.

'This is all wrong, Clem,' he answered hopelessly but with the feeling that he needed to say something in his own defence. 'I never murdered anyone. It's a false charge . . . ' Then he thought about Milly and closed his mouth, for it seemed she left him without argument.

'Well, let's git you back to town,' grunted Burns. 'You kin say what you want to say when we git there.'

'I'm only here as your goddamned prisoner because we need a doctor up at Bluewater!' protested Nick. Then he broke off as he saw his uncle coming into view over the rise.

'You been at Bluewater?' asked Burns suspiciously. 'What the hell for?'

'There's a wounded man there . . . Feather Dan . . . Well, he got shot.'

'Shot? How the hell was thet? You do it?'

'Nope. I can't say who did it. Don't rightly know.' Lying did not come easily to Nick but he felt the need to continue to protect Milly. 'What matters is getting him some help! He needs the doctor and quickly!'

'All right,' decided Burns. 'Hey, Joe, you and Midge git up to Bluewater and find out what's goin' on there. We'll take this feller's word fer it that a doctor is needed and we'll send Doc Cameron whenever we can. Now, let's git goin'!'

Lamprey and Midge sped up the trail towards Bluewater while the rest of the posse turned for home. Robert glared at Nick accusingly but said nothing. Nick stared back with contempt. He was beginning to see something of the snake in his uncle. It surprised him but he was not overwhelmed by amazement.

Robert made for his own office as soon as the party reached town. For the first hour he did no work at all but smoked a cheroot, drank coffee and enjoyed his victory, almost rubbing his hands in glee. Soon all his plans would fall into place and Bluewater would be his and the Mexican silver to boot!

A little further up the street Nick sat in a cell with the sunlight casting dark shadows of iron bars from the window to the floor. Clem Burns looked through the small aperture above the heavy door and shook his head, sad to see Glen Paget's boy reduced to such a level but pleased enough to have the prisoner under lock and key without violence having proved necessary.

'Nick, you've got a helluva lot to answer for but I'll leave the questioning until later when I git everything sorted out. I've sent Doc Cameron up to Bluewater to see to Dan. I jest hope he arrives in time before the old feller dies.

If he's too late there will be hell to pay. Two murders on the same homestead is way over the top. You'll have to tell me all about thet too. Right now jest sit there and think over your position.'

Doc Cameron was a thin, sprightly man who looked younger than his forty years. His little roan took him up the trail very quickly. When he reached the farm he strode purposefully in through the front door in his search for Feather Dan and found himself facing Milly.

'Mrs Paget, I need to see the casualty,' he shouted. 'The man with the gunshot wound, Where is he?'

Milly stared at him from the kitchen door and shrugged her shoulders as if completely baffled by the demand. Cameron stared back into her blood-shot eyes, sighed, and turned back to the porch. Deputy Lamprey was just outside. He motioned towards the little shed a few yards away and Cameron was soon in the dim interior where he stood for a moment in dismay before bending over the patient.

Feather Dan was only semi-conscious. It was evident that he was suffering from shock. The wound, on examination, seemed not to be life-threatening. The bullet had gone right through and had not ripped out an artery or shattered the shoulder-bone. The old man had been lucky . . . so far at any rate. Cameron cleaned up the wound and dressed it in a professional manner, then he went back into the house.

'Mrs Paget, I am going to send a covered cart in from the town to take Dan back there to Mrs Burnett's place. He needs to be nursed properly. He is far too old a man to take a wound like that.'

He felt like adding that the patient needed to be thoroughly washed and the rags he was wearing consigned to the fire if the risk of infection to the wound was to be minimized but he did not say so. He had not seen Milly for years but the change in her appearance shocked him and he made a mental note to give her some attention also when the present crisis was over. He nodded to her courteously and took his leave with a short piece of advice to her to try to relax as much as possible, although he knew he was wasting his breath.

'Look, fellers,' he said to Lamprey and Midge, 'you stick around here and keep an eye on the lady, at least until my cart gets up from the town to take away the Indian. Maybe I can make some arrangement for her to have some female company for the next few days.'

He did not think that was likely for he could not think of any woman who would want to stay with Milly as she now was. It was a poor look-out but she needed help and quickly. That was his professional view.

5

Jayne Heston left home in the early morning on her journey to Pronghorn Flats. Her brothers waved her off; Flint from the paddock and John from a nearby field. There was always work to be done but they showed no resentment at her departure, knowing full well the desire of a young woman to visit town from time to time to buy a new dress or a hat from the store and to talk to her female friends.

They were fond of Jayne and very protective of her but they knew her as a girl of good sense who was not in any way conceited and quite devoid of vanity, although she could not but be aware of her own beauty. She made these visits to the town every few weeks and always stayed quite safely with her friend, Sarah, who lived just off the main street.

Today she rode the big chestnut horse because he was quick and sturdy and, as always, she took with her a small pack-animal to carry her goods back from town. She had, after all, been known to come back with an awkward load of pots and pans, and once with a large clock which had taken her fancy. On this morning, however, the little horse had the lightest of loads as it set off, consisting of two saddle-bags, only one of which contained anything at all, that being an object she had carried out of the house without her brothers being told of it.

In addition she had with her a loaded carbine. She always carried that in case of trouble, although she had not — as yet — ever experienced any. It was a gun she knew how to use.

She arrived in Pronghorn about an hour after the sheriff had come back with Nick Paget. The news had already spread around and Jayne heard it almost as soon as she reached the main street. It seemed Nick's arrest had been as easy as pie and he was now sitting in jail awaiting further investigation prior to the inevitable trial and his certain execution.

The news filled Jayne with dismay and drove all thoughts of her shopping out of her head. She had never ceased to think of Nick since their meeting and one reason for her trip to Pronghorn had been her intention to visit Bluewater, ostensibly to see her old friend, Milly, but just as much to find out whether Nick had ever put in an appearance.

She went to Sarah's house for a time and then wandered back to the vicinity of the sheriff's office. She felt like asking to visit Nick but was sure she would not be allowed to do so. She was in the street when Doctor Cameron returned from Bluewater. She heard him telling Sheriff Burns on the sidewalk of his need to send the cart for Feather Dan and his wish for some female company for Milly. Jayne did not hesitate to offer her services and shortly afterwards she was riding the chestnut and leading her draught animal alongside the doctor's little covered cart, her heart beating hard as she wondered what she would find at Bluewater.

She went into the house as Cameron and his two assistants carried Dan from the dim little hut and placed him gently into the cart. Milly was seated by the window looking out at the neglected garden. She turned her head as Jayne entered and stared for a moment without recognition. Then she smiled and spoke as if they had parted the day before.

'Hullo, Jayne, how are you? Fine day out but hot, ain't it.'

'It's so good to see you, Milly,' answered Jayne, taken aback for a few seconds by the terrible change for the worse that she saw in her friend. 'You're looking fine . . . ' She wondered what to say next but smiled brightly. 'What are you doing today?'

'Nothing much.'

'Have you seen Nick?' Jayne asked

the question with some trepidation, feeling that she might have mentioned his name too soon. 'I heard he was here.'

'He went away. Going back East or somewhere maybe . . . '

'He was always a fine boy, Milly. Always fond of you too. I always reckoned he was a real gentleman. He could never have hurt anybody.'

'No.'

'Remember how he painted your picture, Milly? He captured all your beauty. I have it here.' Jayne unwrapped the flat rectangular parcel she had carried in her saddle-bag. 'See, here it is! Remember you rescued it from the field and then later gave it to me to look after because of what Glen would think?'

Milly stared at the painting, eyes widening, then she smiled, her expression one of extreme pleasure.

'God, it's me! He made me beautiful!'

'He just painted what he saw, Milly.

You're still beautiful! But do you know what they want to do to that fine boy, Milly? They want to do something terrible. They don't want him to live! They say he did a terrible thing, but he didn't — did he, Milly?'

'It's a lovely picture, ain't it?'

'Sure, it is, Milly. See here where there are real flower-petals in the corner. That was because the paint was still wet when Glen threw it into the field and it fell amongst the flowers They're all set into it now but they still have their colours — hardly faded at all.'

'They must have been growing then, when I was so young and beautiful! That was before . . . well, before . . . '

'Nick didn't do anything bad, did he, Milly? We need to tell the truth so that he goes on living and painting. He'll paint you again too, I'm certain of that! Tell me what really happened that day. Nothing bad will happen to you . . . '

It was not quite true. Jayne knew that as she spoke but she could not have

Nick condemned as a murderer, knowing him to be innocent. She could see in Milly's eyes the fear of the rope. There was guilt in the woman's mind and with it a terror that seemed to scream silently forth. Regardless of what might have happened, Milly would not hang. They must treat her and bring her back to complete sanity. After that — well they would take care of her, as they must. Whatever they did, it must be better than the injustice of hanging an innocent man.

'Nick did not kill Glen, did he, Milly?'

'No. Well, I don't remember! It was all mixed up and Glen's brother said there would be a hanging! It was murder! Then he saw Nick riding up to the farm. He told the sheriff! Then there was Dan. He said the same. He saw the whole thing. It wasn't me at all — it was Nick! Even Robert said that!'

'It was not Nick, Milly! You can't say that! We can't tell lies about him. Do you remember how he used to paint such fine pictures and how much you admired him? He was your friend. You were such good friends!'

Milly collapsed over the table, weeping. Her hands drummed on the wooden top.

'I don't know — I just don't know! It's all a mix up! I don't want to hang!'

'That won't ever happen, Milly!' Jayne's arms were about the distraught woman's shoulders. 'Nothing bad will happen if we tell the truth.'

Lamprey was looking in from the door, an anxious expression on his long face.

'You all right, Miss Heston? Me and Midge is still here.'

Jayne got up and went into the porch. Both men looked uncomfortable, Lamprey was shuffling his feet nervously.

'Thing is, Miss Heston, we need to be getting back. Don't think the sheriff meant us to stay too long. But you need to keep a sharp look-out. Make sure she — Mrs Paget — don't git her hands on anything like a knife or somethin'. She don't seem right, you know . . . '

'It'll be all right. You two just go when it suits you. Milly and I . . . ' she added loudly, 'are old friends!'

So it was that the two deputies rode back to Pronghorn somewhat uneasily, both wondering at the wisdom of leaving the young girl in the company of what seemed to them to be a madwoman. When they reached the office of Clem Burns, they found him very thoughtful. He informed them that the prisoner had told him he had been living in a place called Deal out East and that his employer and friends there could vouch for his whereabouts at the time of Glen's death. He also knew a lot of people in the town and even the name of the gunsmith's horse that he used to ride sometimes. The only thing was he had used the name of Munro so as to make a complete break with his former life but folks would vouch for him just the same. Also, he sounded real convincing, which in itself was disturbing.

The sheriff spent some time writing up a report and later in the afternoon looked up in surprise when Doctor Cameron came into the office.

'I was jest coming round to see you,' remarked Burns. 'Thought I'd give you time to see the patient settled. How is Dan?'

'Dead,' replied Cameron. 'The whole thing has been too much of a shock for an old man.'

'Jeeze, well, what do we have here, another murder or what?'

'Dan said it was an accident. He fell over the rifle when he was carrying it.'

'Yeah? Well. The wound will be in his front and there must be burn marks on his clothes from such close range. I'll need to see the clothes.'

'They've been put in the fire. Mrs Burnett says they were filthy and covered in fleas. I believe it. She didn't think they were any good to keep.'

'Christ, that's it then. Evidence all gone.'

'Yeah, and Dan said a few things

before he slipped off. He said *he* killed Glen Paget. He claims that Glen and him had a stinking row and Glen called him an Indian dog so Dan let him have it with a gun. Says he was too scared to admit it before but not when he knew he was dying. He was real sorry he had told all them lies about that decent, kind young feller and didn't believe either the story Robert Paget told about seeing Nick in the neighbourhood. It was a real confession.'

'Death-bed confession,' grunted Burns, amazed. 'Think he was telling the truth?'

'Hard to say. That's for you and the law to decide.'

'Death-bed confessions are generally held to be true. Christians are careful what they stay before passing over.'

'He wasn't thet,' put in Lamprey from the other side of the room. 'He was still all Injun . . . but, as fer Christians, they're few and far between, I ain't never met any.'

They looked at him sharply. Lamprey, for all his sharp-shooting and the number of outlaws he had sent to boot hill, thought of himself as a man who tried to live a Christian life, though he never claimed to have achieved it.

'I'm going up to Bluewater,' growled Burns, exasperated. 'I need to question that woman a bit more.'

He came back in the evening and opened up the cell door so that Nick could get out. Robert Paget had dropped into the office just at that moment, eager to find out how the investigation was going. Burns looked round at him in surprise.

'You'll be pleased to hear, Mr Paget, thet we have nothin' on your nephew and are letting him go,' he stated, with the faintest trace of irony in his tone. 'Thet woman up at the farm is as mixed up as hell. One minute she says maybe Nick did it then she says maybe he didn't, maybe it was a stranger, then she thinks maybe there *was* no stranger. When I asked if Feather Dan might have done it, she says, yeah, maybe he did it or for sure he did it . . . A woman as mixed up as thet is of no more use as a witness than a goddamned mocking-bird. Thet's for sure!'

'But she was certain before!' objected Robert.

'Well, she sure ain't now! Anyway, now we have Feather Dan claiming thet he did it and he's gone and died on us so we can't question him any further. Still it's a confession and can't be ignored.'

'You can't take seriously two people like that! A half-crazy woman and an old Indian who hardly knew what day of the week it was!'

'We did before, Mr Paget, and you were in favour then.'

'Remember, I saw Nick Paget in the neighbourhood at the time.'

'So you said, but you could easy have seen somebody who jest happened to look a bit like him and, according to the young feller, he's got plenty of witnesses in this place called Deal who will swear he was in thet town all the time. Thet can be checked out but there ain't no doubt in my mind thet they'll support him. Anyway, we jest have nothin' on him and I'm letting him go.'

Nick walked out of the sheriff's office in a daze, truly amazed to find himself suddenly at liberty. He did not look at his uncle but went straight for the grey horse still hitched by the sidewalk.

'Where are you heading, Nick?' asked Lamprey from the street.

'Back to Bluewater, I guess,' answered Nick. 'I want to see Milly.'

'Miss Heston is there as well,' Lamprey informed him.

Nick was surprised and pleased to hear it. He put his heels to the old grey and headed out of town on the road he had taken as a prisoner not so long before.

Minutes later, Robert Paget left town also, on the swift black, and took another route in the direction of Bluecoat Ridge. He scowled in fury as he went and forced Midnight into a gallop which even a strong horse could not have sustained for long. When he came near his own farm he took another path into wild country of rugged slopes and ugly distorted trees. After some hours, during which the tired horse was forced to slow down, he found himself in a landscape that was flattening out into wide grassland. This he knew was the start of cattle country. He could see a long way ahead into a featureless prairie and it was then that he began to regret his impulse to start on such a journey without proper planning and at the wrong time of day.

As darkness fell, he was obliged to dismount and try to sleep in the grass while the horse rested nearby. He had nothing to eat or drink and sleeping outside was something he had not done since his boyhood, when he had sometimes gone on hunting trips with his brother. He had a bad night and arose stiff and sore as dawn broke. The black was well rested and had eaten its fill of grass and was, therefore, in much better shape than he was. He went on doggedly just the same, his mind full of the need to meet up with Jed Brandt who, he knew, had a cabin not so far ahead, nearby the Buckweed River.

About half-way through the forenoon, he saw the cabin in the distance under one of the very few clumps of trees to be found. When he reached it, he discovered nobody there but an old cowpuncher, smoking a pipe and nursing a strained knee. When Robert asked about Brandt the old man waved his arm towards the river, which could just be seen some distance away, gleaming in the sun.

Robert was very weary when a few cowhands, rounding up strays, came into view. To his relief, he recognized Brandt on a small rise, directing operations.

'Am I glad to see you, Jed,' panted Robert, smiling a little ingratiatingly. 'I need to talk business.'

Brandt looked at Robert but did not allow his astonishment to show in his expression. Men dressed in city suits were seldom seen on a cattle drive. He grinned through his thick black beard, showing a fine set of teeth.

'Yeah? Well, this *is* a surprise, Mr Paget.' He had no liking for Robert Paget but recognized that, as a lawyer, and not always such a straight one, he might have his uses. 'What kin I do fer you?'

Robert leaned over the neck of the black, his face showing exhaustion.

'Look, Jed, before we start, I'm starving! Have you anything to eat? I haven't drunk anything either since God knows when.'

'Ain't got nothin'.' Brandt grinned. 'And if you want a drink — there's the river.'

'I didn't ride out all this way just to drink out of the goddamned river!' ejaculated Robert. 'Anyhow, can we dismount? I have a few ideas to put to you.'

They sat some distance away from the other men, well out of earshot.

Brandt filled his pipe and listened attentively while Robert explained about the return of Nick, his arrest and his subsequent release as the result of the only witnesses changing their story. Brandt grinned sardonically and spat into the grass but made no comment. Robert looked at him quizzically, wondering what was in the cattleman's mind but could not guess. He felt, nevertheless, that he had no option but to trust this man.

'Anyhow,' he said eventually, 'that's why I'm here, Jed. I need some help from you.'

'Yeah?'

'I need you to see to things for me. I need Bluewater Farm but right now that sister-in-law of mine and my nephew stand in the way. The legal position is that she inherits the place and after she goes, whenever the hell that is, Nick takes over. He could outlive me by God knows how long. I'll just level with you, Jed, I want them out of the way and it needs to be permanent.'

'You mean killing them?'

'Sure, it's the only way.'

'That goddamned farm means all that to you?'

'Yeah, I always wanted it and I must have it now.'

'Not much in the way of family love, heh?' Brandt grinned sarcastically.

Robert did not rise to the remark, which nettled him, but smiled a little as he shrugged his shoulders.

'That don't come into it. Thing is, Jed, will you help me in this? I'll make it worth your while.'

'How much?'

'A thousand dollars.'

'Thet's for the woman — how much for the young feller?'

Robert curbed an impulse to swear.

'All right, the same again for him.'

'You must want that damned farm pretty bad.'

Brandt mused for a moment. He remembered his meeting with Glen Paget and the talk about buying hundreds of head of cattle. There had suddenly been money about where there had been none before. He had thought quite a lot about that since then and had pricked up his ears when he had heard about Glen's sudden death, by all accounts at the hand of his own son. Money did not suddenly fall out of the sky to please hard-working farmers. The old stories about old man Busby and his team of heavily laden mules had come back to him.

The story Brandt had heard was that there had been about eight mules just about breaking their backs with Mexican silver, all in coin, that the sly feller had stolen during the war. There was no way Busby had ever spent it. That meant it had been hidden away someplace and Glen's sudden prosperity indicated that he had found it.

And here was this smart lawyer ready to pay to have his own relatives murdered. It could only mean the Mexican booty was on the farm which was why this polecat was ready to go to any lengths to get his hands on the place.

'All right, Paget, I'll do it,' agreed Brandt, 'but you send somebody up here tomorrow with the money, then I'll move.'

They shook hands on the deal. Robert felt relieved. Brandt grinned, his mind on the Mexican silver which he had no intentions of allowing ever to fall into the hands of the sly little man he was dealing with.

6

Marty Philps lay with his eyes closed on the rough bunk and listened to the voices outside. It was very late for him to be still in bed but he had scarcely slept all night. Usually, he would have been up at dawn to begin work with rounding up strays or branding calves but not today. His badly sprained knee had seen to that. He believed it would keep him from work for about a week, which meant he would be out of a job pretty soon. He was getting old anyway and he was well aware that his boss, Jed Brandt, had been thinking of getting rid of him.

The voices outside were faint because of the wooden walls of the bunkhouse but he could just about make out the gist of the conversation. Jed Brandt was giving his foreman, Willis, instructions, not about the day's work, but about something else which had to do with the lawyer, Paget, and Bluewater Farm and the rounding up of a few of the boys who could be trusted.

Marty knew that to *be trusted*, in Brandt's mind, was to be capable of taking part in some activity outside the law. He knew that because he, himself, had been in that position when he had been younger and fitter and able to pull a gun without worrying too much about the legality of it.

Now, he had to admit, he was past all that and Jed Brandt knew it and did not trust him in any such way at all. For some years, Marty had been good for poking cattle and branding calves but not anything else. Now he couldn't do that either and since Jed Brandt did not pay anybody for laying around sick, pretty soon he would be starving as well and then sent on his way without a cent in the pocket of his greasy old jacket.

Although he could not make out every word of Brandt's conversation with Willis, he was piecing it together quite well. In addition to the mention of Bluewater and doing something about the young feller and the half-crazy woman there, he had heard Brandt say something about Mexican silver. Marty knew as much as anybody did about old Busby's silver-laden mules. He had heard all the stories long before Brandt ever had. He had observed the serious conversation between Brandt and Paget the day before and guessed that the rider he had heard approaching a short while ago had come from him. The rider had gone off very quickly but almost certainly he had brought money with him because Brandt never did anything for anyone unless he was well paid.

His mind went back to the visit Brandt had had from Glen Paget and the talk of a big cattle deal that had spilled out to the cowhands, although it never took place because Glen had not lived long enough to see it through. Like Brandt, Marty was quite capable of fitting all that together and making the shrewd guess that Glen had suddenly got his hands on his dead father's silver hoard.

Marty listened as two horses galloped away in different directions and knew that Brandt and Willis were riding out to round up the men they needed. He lay until he reckoned they were out of sight, then hauled himself painfully out of the dirty bunk and made for the door. Outside there was nothing but grass and the glint of the river in the distance. The only living thing to be seen was his old sorrel munching at the grass and a raven searching for something to eat round the embers of the camp-fire. The raven was about as hungry as he was. The cabin was used from time to time only, depending on where they were doing the branding, and was not well provided with rations. Marty knew that the last of the coffee had been drunk by the cowhands early that morning before they rode off.

Hunger, though, was not such an unusual experience for him, nor was pain, as he had broken a few bones in his body over the years, so he saddled his horse and rode away from the empty camp with scarcely a grimace even though his knee felt as if the hound dog that had been gnawing at it all night was determined not to give up.

He rode in the direction of Bluecoat Ridge. The farm lay at a long distance but he did not much care about that, as he had no intentions of retracing his steps. In a sense, he thought, it was hardly out of his way.

He reached the farm about midday and the first thing he noticed was the lawyer feller walking up and down in front of the house, looking agitated and slapping his hands on his sides, almost as if he felt cold although the weather was warm enough to cook eggs on the stones.

'Howdy!' called Marty in gruff cheerfulness. 'Fine day, ain't it!'

Robert Paget stopped his nervous pacing and looked round in surprise. He had an idea he might have seen the old man the day before but was not sure. He grunted a reply, scowling as he did so. He did not like rough old cowhands looking in on him, and especially not now when he was sick with worry.

The truth was that doubts as to the wisdom of employing Jed Brandt to do his dirty work had crept into his mind during the night. It was not beyond a man like Brandt to keep the money and simply refuse to do the job at all. For that reason, Robert had sent a note along with the $2,000 in which he offered a greatly increased reward when the task of disposing of certain parties was actually accomplished. That, he hoped, would do the trick and ensure Brandt's full cooperation. Even so, he was by no means certain that he could count on Brandt and the idea had been burning up his brain since before dawn.

'Mr Paget,' grinned Marty, showing a set of bad teeth through his grey beard, 'I've got some information fer you that I reckon is worth every cent of fifty dollars. I'll give it to ya straight. Jed Brandt knows full well thet old Busby's silver has been found and is up at Bluewater and he reckons on gittin' it and keeping it fer himself. Whatever else you asked him to do he might do — or he might not — fer all I know, but the one thing he's planning fer sure is to git his hands on thet old Mexican silver. Now thet bit of information is worth fifty dollars of your money. If you think it ain't, then I'll do a double-cross on you thet will make Jed Brandt look like he oughta be teaching Sunday school.'

Robert gaped, his mouth falling loosely under his lank moustache. Although he had begun to suspect that he might be cheated by Brandt, it had not occurred to him that the cattleman could have figured out that the silver was at Bluewater, and within reach after Nick and his stepmother had been dealt with. If that idea was in his mind then there was no doubt he would try for it; nor could there be any doubt now that he *did* know about it. If this old cowpoke knew then it was a certainty that Jed Brandt knew also.

He stared for a full minute at Marty, hardly seeing the old man's grin and penetrating glance. Robert's mind was in turmoil. He felt at a complete loss as to what to do. In his heart he cursed himself for a fool to involve a man like Brandt.

'Fifty dollars, mister,' growled Marty.

The words woke Robert out of his daze. It went against the grain to hand fifty dollars to a man who looked no different from a saddle-tramp but he felt that Marty's threat of a massive double-cross might be true. The one thing he wanted to avoid at the present time was the making of more enemies.

Without another word, Robert went into the house where he opened the strongbox he kept bolted to the floor in his bedroom and took out fifty dollars. He passed the money silently to Marty who grinned and thrust the notes into his pocket.

'Thanks, mister,' said the old man. 'I sure appreciate it. Best of luck with Jed Brandt — you'll need it!'

Marty jerked his sorrel into a trot and took the trail to the north-west, where he believed he might still have friends.

For some time Robert stood in utter silence by the fence then he turned and went into his house where he sat and stared at a picture of cattlemen driving a herd towards the sunset. He did not see it. His mind was entirely focused on Brandt and what the double-crossing skunk would do next. It did not take much figuring out. An armed gang would go to Bluewater — maybe in the dark — kill Nick and Milly, and then spend as long as it took to ransack the place and come up with the silver. Brandt and maybe one of his trusted lieutenants would share the hoard between them, while their followers would very likely be paid off with the $2,000 provided by courtesy of Mr Robert Paget.

The first part of the plan was as it should be but the second part must not be allowed to happen. How could it be prevented? Robert writhed in his chair as his mind jumped from one possibility to the next.

Meanwhile, Brandt and Willis were riding over different parts of the range, searching for the men Jed had already selected. It took much of the day as the individuals concerned were widely scattered. In the evening five men besides Brandt and Willis sat by a lonely fire to work out details of the plan. Willis suggested that an attack under cover of darkness would be the best plan but Brandt decided that to move in at dawn would be preferable. They needed some light to see by and their victims would likely be still asleep.

'Injun attack, heh?' grinned Pert, wiping his long nose on the back of his hand. 'Scalp them afore they git their eyes open!'

'No need fer no scalpin'!' snapped Brandt, in no mood for jokes. 'Couple of bullets should do it.'

Pert was the kind of man who would have killed his grandmother for ten dollars. Brandt had chosen him for his ruthlessness. Few men, no matter how used to killing, liked the idea of murdering a woman but Pert had no such compunctions. He could be depended upon to take care of Mrs Paget. Brandt was more than willing to settle the young feller, Nick, himself but he needed a few guns along just in case things started to unravel.

'When?' asked Bo Hart, scratching his long hair.

Brandt edged back a little from him. He lit his pipe and then said evenly:

'At dawn, like I said.'

'Which dawn, for Chris'sake?' growled Pert.

Brandt held his temper. He had already made up his mind that some of the present company would not be around to share in the proceeds of this raid. Certainly the Mexican silver was for himself and maybe Willis. The others must be sent away with Paget's money but that would depend on their survival. It seemed to Brandt that whether or not they survived would be dependent upon how he, Brandt, felt about it at the time. It was a sure thing that Pert would end up with a bullet.

'Not tomorrow,' he decided. 'Day after — but at first light. We're resting tomorrow. We've been riding all god-damned day, so get some rest and make sure you keep off the booze.'

There was no booze but he said that just to irritate Pert who liked his liquor. Not that it made much sense to annoy Pert right now but he was an irritating polecat and already getting on Brandt's nerves.

The dawn raid, he reflected, was the best bet. After the killing was over there would be plenty of hours of daylight to search for the silver. If he could find it without the rest of the gang knowing so much the better because then he would try to send them away with Paget's money while he carried off old Busby's loot. If there was a lot of it then he would need the help of his men to load it on to a wagon or any spare horses they could find. Later, he would get rid of Pert and the others in his own way — Willis too, in all probability. He had seen that kind of thing done before; two guys shoot three in the back — one guy shoots the other — the boss steps in and shoots the survivor and winner takes all.

Night fell. The gang wrapped themselves in their blankets and fell asleep by the embers of the fire. Brandt lay awake and watched the moon as it rose and illuminated the grassland. He had seen it many times before but now it seemed to him to be like a gigantic silver peso floating in the sky. He had never been a romantic but it looked more beautiful to him tonight than it ever had.

At about the same time as Brandt was discussing matters with his followers, Robert Paget was saddling up Midnight and packing a small amount of provisions to carry with him.

The task ahead filled him with gloom and trepidation. After the departure of Marty, he had sat for a long time in his own front room trying to think of some way of preventing Jed Brandt from getting his hands on the silver. In the end he had come up with a plan which had as many snags and holes as a mountain stream but was no worse than the one he had already set in motion with Jed Brandt.

Not far from the boundary of his own property a brook ran down the ridge and followed a winding course through the woodland for many miles. It came out very close to the trail that stretched between Bluewater and Pronghorn Flats. There was a track alongside the waterway that was just wide enough to take a horse and Robert reckoned that if he set off at dusk he would emerge from the trees a couple of hours before dawn. At that point he would be within a mile or a mile and a half of Bluewater Farm and, in the silence of the night, within earshot of any gunfire. When he heard that first shot, he aimed to ride like hell into Pronghorn on the fastest horse he had ever known and rouse up Sheriff Burns and his deputies to investigate.

He hoped that they would reach the farm too late to save Milly and Nick but before Jed Brandt could get his hands on the Mexican silver. He believed it might just work. It would not take the gang long to complete the killings but it was likely that they would have some trouble locating the loot.

He himself had no clear idea where the stuff was hidden. On his visits to Bluewater after the death of his brother he had never once heard Milly make mention of it. He had taken care not to mention it to her because the last thing he wanted was to have her doing something foolish with it. It was, after all, her legal property. He had concluded that Glen had kept the existence of the silver a secret from his wife and had it hidden, either in old Busby's original hiding-place or in one of his own. It could take a lot of searching for but he had no doubt that he would find it, given time and his determination to turn the entire place over if necessary.

A shoot-out with the sheriff and his men would certainly put a sudden end to Brandt's hopes. It might even finish the outlaw, which would keep him from attempting to incriminate Robert, although there was little chance of the sheriff giving any credence to the protestations of a cornered criminal.

As he rode through the trees, Robert led a saddleless horse behind him. It was his alibi in the sense that it provided an excuse for his riding about at such a strange hour. Sheriff Burns might well ask him the question and Robert was ready to say that he had, naturally enough, gone in search of the animal, which had strayed from his farm, but he had allowed his anxiety to lead him too far into the night.

In addition to the spare horse, he had with him a few provisions and a flask of cold coffee. He had a feeling that he might be out in the open for many hours, a thought that made him want to spit, for he was not one who enjoyed the night air and the darkness. Not that the night was so very dark, as he discovered when the moon came up and filtered through the branches overhead.

Maybe Brandt would decide to do the job by moonlight! It was a possibility and that might mean it could all begin to happen long before Robert ever got clear of the woods. There was nothing else for it, however, but to keep on going and hope for the best.

As he went, his mind kept going back to Glen and Milly. Their marriage had been a disaster from day one but it need not have ended in the way it had, with Glen lying in the yard with a bullet through the brain. Robert had happened to arrive at the farm before the sheriff or anybody else had got wind of the murder. Robert knew the real culprit but had spent a great deal of time trying to make certain that the blame fell upon Nick. He had sat at the kitchen table for many an hour sympathizing with Milly and emphasizing the need for her to keep to the story that a man who looked just like Nick — who was, he eventually persuaded her, in fact Nick — had ridden in and shot Glen for no other reason than some sense of grievance.

He had also talked quite a lot about the gallows and how Nick would certainly finish up having his neck stretched, as would any murderer, no matter what possible reasons for losing one's temper and going for a gun might be thought about.

He had seen Milly cringe and withdraw into herself as fear swept through her and knew she would stick to her story. She had, too, until that lunatic Indian had started singing his goddamned death song and making peace with the world before he left it. At least, that was the only reason for the change in her testimony that Robert could think of. It had been enough to really mess everything up, which was why he was making his way through the woods in the middle of the night with twigs hitting him in the face and his eyes beginning to droop for want of sleep.

After a couple of miles, he let the spare horse go. The fact that it was wandering was good enough to support his story and it was troublesome to lead it on the narrow track where it was forever pulling back and snorting. He made better time after that and reached the further end of the woods shortly before a streak of grey appeared in the east.

So far there had been no sound of a gunshot. It was with relief that he halted in the shelter of the thinning trees and looked out over the trail that led to Bluewater. He dismounted and sat down to drink a little cold coffee and eat a sandwich. It might be some time before he heard anything but when he did he was determined to mount up in double-quick time and ride with all speed into town. Midnight was still fresh as he had been going at no more than walking pace and another half-hour or so of rest would set him racing. Later on in the day, when there was time, Midnight would dine on the oats Robert thoughtfully carried with him. He loved that horse. He had to admit it. It was the only living thing he had any regard for.

Dawn came to the accompaniment of birdsong in the surrounding woods. Robert listened carefully for the sound of a shot but heard none. The sun rose and bathed the world in light. The nearest part of the trail to Bluewater was quite clear and the grass-covered hillside beyond it gave off a faint mist as the dew of the night evaporated. There was no living thing to be seen from his vantage point but flying birds and a few dairy cattle dozing in the grass.

Robert sighed. Had he been wrong to assume that Brandt would make a dawn attack? Was it possible that he might move in on the farm during the daylight hours? There was no telling with a man like Brandt. With every moment that passed Robert regretted more the impulse that had made him seek help from such an unreliable character.

All day he waited, keeping out of sight amid the trees, but seeing no one on the trail and hearing no sound of gunfire. It occurred to him that young Nick might decide to leave Bluewater that day and head back East. If he did it really would mess everything up. The chances were, though, that he would spend a day or two with his stepmother, who needed someone to steady her nerves. Then, being in the clear as far as the law was concerned, he would travel by coach from the town for such a journey. If he did not appear on the trail then he would certainly be still at the farm. It was the one little bit of comfort to be extracted from the miserable day.

Night fell and Robert struggled to remain awake. Midnight was restless and he had to make sure the horse was well tethered to a sapling. From time to time Robert fell asleep for a moment or two, then awoke with a start, cursing under his breath.

Early in the morning of his second night in the woods, he heard a far-off shot. Stiffly he rose to his feet, breathing hard in his excitement, mounted, and rode like the wind for Pronghorn Flats.

7

Nick lay awake as the first hint of light came into the sky. It had been his third night at Bluewater since his release and he had not slept any better than he had on the first. The intervening days had been difficult. To begin with, Milly had been in a fraught state of mind and he and Jayne had spent much time seeking to calm her. They had succeeded to a certain extent by speaking in a friendly and encouraging way to her and repeatedly stating that they believed Feather Dan's story of how he had killed Glen on that fateful day. Gradually, it seemed that she believed it too and fear went from her eyes so that she smiled and even joked a little with Nick and put her arms around Jayne in sisterly affection.

Such had been the state of affairs when they eventually retired, Nick to a made-up bed in the parlour and the two women to the bedroom. As the night went on, however, Nick had lain awake, his mind full of the knowledge that the old Indian had not been the murderer. Milly had said enough in her ravings to convince him of that. He knew too, that he had nothing to say to the law over the matter. It seemed to him that in some situations, the victim of violence might become so distressed that to strike back can seem the only recourse . . .

Milly had spoken a lot about her brother-in-law, Robert, also. He it was who had warned her about the looming gallows and had first mentioned Nick, whom he claimed to have seen nearby. It was all becoming plain enough to Nick. His uncle wanted him and Milly out of the way and Glen's death had seemed the right opportunity to achieve that without seeming to go outside the law.

Why? Could it be that Robert was so keen on inheriting Bluewater that he would go to such lengths? Somehow that did not ring true.

There came the sound of a horse snorting from some distance away. It was too far off to have been one of the four horses now in the nearby paddock. There were no others on the land round about as far as Nick was aware. He lay for a moment, listening for the sound to be repeated but all was silent.

Nevertheless, there was a sense of danger. His own heightened state of nerves after his recent ordeal made the feeling acute. He rose silently and drew on his pants and his gunbelt. Then he slipped on his boots. Very slowly and quietly he moved to the window. The yard outside was just beginning to reveal itself in soft grey light. He stared across it to the dark outline of the barn and a stretch of fencing which vanished into the murk. Then he gasped. A figure moved forward, climbed easily over the fence and crept silently to the corner of the barn.

'Nick, what is it?' Jayne was beside

him, her hand touching his arm. 'I thought I heard something.'

She spoke in an apprehensive whisper. He twisted round and pressed the fingers of his left hand on to hers. In his right, he held the Colt .45. In his mind was Robert, the smart lawyer, the clever liar, and the man who wanted him dead and Milly driven out of her mind or, if needs be, on the end of a rope.

He realized suddenly that Jayne was too near the window. Her face could catch the faint light and show up through the glass.

'Down a little,' he whispered, but he was too late. There came the crack of a handgun and the glass pane shattered, sending a shower of splinters over them both. She fell on to the boards. He ducked too but was up again in an instant. There was a figure still there, half-concealed in the shadows. Nick thrust his gun through the gap in the glass and fired. There came a yelp of pain and a curse and the vague figure disappeared. Suddenly there came a savage burst of gunfire. Bullets smashed through the window at the other end of the room and embedded themselves in the wall. Nick crouched and at the same time twisted round to look for Jayne. She had vanished and he felt relieved that she had sought shelter in the other room, but then she returned, almost crawling on the floor to keep below the level of the windows. In her hands she held the carbine. He noticed she still wore the blue nightdress lent to her by Milly and her feet were bare.

Nick looked again out of the window from which he had fired. There was no sign of life. Beyond the dark shadows of the outbuildings there was nothing to be seen but the lightening sky.

At the other end of the parlour Jayne lifted her head to look through the glass. To her horror, she saw two men running towards the house from the stable block, guns in hand, ready to send a fusillade of bullets into the room. She did not hesitate. The carbine came up, smashed through the glass and fired almost as one movement. The foremost man fell with no sound but the clatter of his gun as it hit the stones. The other one scampered to one side and threw himself to the ground as he sought shelter behind a horse trough.

The man who had fallen lay still. Jayne knew he had taken the bullet through the heart. She felt nothing. It was as if she had shot a wolf rushing towards her. The overwhelming sense of danger drove out all emotion. She had no feeling of triumph or anger or fear. She was aware only of a heightening of her own senses that brought an ice-coolness into her mind and a steady hand on her gun.

Outside, in the half dark, Jed Brandt crouched behind a low wall, biting his lip, his still unfired Colt ready in his hand. He knew Whitey was dead and Pert was trying to stem blood streaming from the graze in his arm. Things were not going at all as Brandt had expected. The young guy ought to have been dead by now and the woman either dead or awaiting a quick bullet. He wondered how many people were in the farmhouse. A handgun had wounded Pert and it was pretty certain, to judge by the report, that Whitey had been downed by a cavalry rifle. That meant two guns, both pretty effective. He pondered for a moment and then winced as he heard the unmistakable boom of a Winchester. Christ, who was in that building? For a second he wondered if the law had got wind of Paget's plan and a posse was in the house, but he dismissed the idea at once. The sheriff would certainly have spread his men out to ambush the raiders instead of confining them in a situation from which no ambush was possible.

It seemed, nevertheless, that there were at least three armed men in the building. Dealing with them was likely to be expensive. They could shoot from their position of advantage and kill several of his men before they were overpowered. If the only possible reward in all of this had been Robert Paget's money, Brandt would have called the attack off there and then. It was only the promise of the Mexican silver that kept him there. In his mind's eye, he still saw old Busby leading his string of mules laden with treasure. He would not give up but he had to act quickly. He stared at the farmhouse in the morning light, knowing that with every moment his men must become more visible while the defenders could keep out of sight.

Nick and Jayne had heard the sound of the Winchester also and knew Milly had found ammunition and had joined battle. It was apparent that she had fired from the little window of the bedroom. It was a tiny window, unglazed, but could be closed with a single wooden shutter — all right for taking a potshot but providing a very limited field of view. The fact, though, that she was aware of the attackers and was prepared to defend herself was encouraging.

Neither Jayne nor Nick moved from their respective positions by the parlour windows. They did not dare go through to the bedroom to see Milly but had to keep a close look-out at all times. Then they heard a door and knew she had entered the kitchen. There was a second door there, leading to the back of the house. It was on the same side as Nick was overlooking and he waited anxiously, hoping with all his heart that she would not go out.

Such an idea was not in Milly's mind at that moment. Her heart pounded with fear and she felt she should hide in order to save her own life. She had fired the Winchester at a shadow, believing it to be Sheriff Burns who had come with his men to arrest her. There was, however, no hiding-place that she could think of. All she could do was to shoot at them and go on shooting until they were all dead and she might be left alone.

The kitchen seemed a better place from which to fight. The walls were of solid stone and could stop the bullets. Also, she could see her enemies coming by looking over the sink and through the wide window.

She had scarcely entered the kitchen, however, when she heard rustling and scrambling sounds. The dark figure of a man appeared, hauling himself up and pushing at the shutter. In a moment, he was inside and had one leg over the sink. In his hand he held a Colt.

Milly did not hesitate. In her state of mind she was incapable of such hesitation. The man was too close for her to train the barrel of the rifle upon him but her hand sought the carving knife, always to be found on the dresser, and plunged it into his neck. He died, sprawling half in the window, with blood pouring from his throat on to his outstretched leg and into the sink.

She stood and watched him die. It was as if she stood by the gallows and watched him swing . . .

Jed Brandt had seen Rusty Smith

climb in the kitchen window and saw him slump as he came to his sudden end. Brandt cursed Rusty as a reckless fool, always out to show how smart he was. Now he had paid the penalty, although by what means, Brandt could only guess. This kind of attack, like a bunch of drunken Indians, made no sense. He must think of another plan.

'Hey, Jed,' Bo Hart had appeared beside him, with an oil-lamp in his hands. 'Found this in thet old shed over there. Let's burn the rats out. We kin shoot them as they run.'

It was the best idea yet. If it was thrown into the right place it could create a fire that must send the defenders scampering.

'Thet lamp filled with oil?'

'Yeah, and there's more. I got the canister here. We kin throw it all in together!'

'Thet's it,' breathed Brandt. 'You got it, Bo! You goin' to throw it?'

It was a dangerous assignment.

'What's in it fer me?' asked Bo.

'Two thousand dollars,' offered Brandt, feeling certain he would never be called upon to pay it.

'It's a deal,' agreed Bo. 'Keep their goddamned heads down until I get in close.'

Brandt gave the signal and bullets poured through the windows. Bo made his way with extreme caution round to the gable end of the house where there were no windows. Just around the corner was the window from which Jayne had fired. The glass had been smashed and Bo knew it was possible to swing the lamp up to the open space and hurl it into the room. He lit the lamp and carried it carefully in his right hand while his left held the opened canister of kerosene. As he turned the corner he kept his body as low as possible. He waited for a second more until his comrades had put another couple of shots into the room and then he darted forward and threw both objects with all his might in through the window.

Within a very few seconds a sheet of flame spread across the carpet and the table. Flames began to lick at the old upholstered chair. A basket nearby began to burn.

'My God!' exclaimed Jayne, backing away, fearful that her nightdress might catch fire.

'We need to get out of here!' shouted Nick. 'The whole room will go up!'

They retreated to the little porch, slamming the door behind them. The kitchen door stood open and they hurried in, seeing it as a temporary place of refuge. Milly stood stock still, looking towards the sink. They gasped as they caught sight of the hideous, bloody corpse with its one leg dangling and blood-soaked clothes.

Milly turned as they entered. Her eyes were empty for a few seconds then they seemed to come alive as if in sudden realization. She turned from them and pushed open the outside door. Then she was out in the yard, nightdress rippling in the light breeze, rifle still in hand.

'Glen! Glen!' she screamed. 'Glen! Look out, Glen!'

She raised the rifle and fired wildly. The bullet hit the ground but she ran on, still screaming, while Nick ran after her, appealing to her to return.

It was too late. Pert, his mind seething with the pain of the graze from Nick's Colt, full of intense anger and hatred, stepped from behind a wall and fired his revolver. The bullet went into her stomach and she lurched forward, rifle clattering to the ground. She was on her knees, but Pert fired again, his bullet smashing through her shoulder-bone. A swift third slug entered her head and she fell her full length on the stones.

Pert grinned but then ducked as Nick fired his Colt. The bullet missed Pert but a shot from Jayne's carbine took out his knee-cap and sent him scrambling in agony for the shelter of the granite wall.

Nick turned to look at her and saw

her almost as a silhouette against the burning building. The heat struck his face and he knew that to return to the kitchen even for a few precious minutes would be to leap into a trap of no return.

'Come on!' he yelled, gripping her arm. 'This way!'

'But Milly! What about Milly?'

'We can't do anything. Come with me!'

They ran past Milly's still form and Nick snatched up the Winchester as they went. He led Jayne out past the wall and a shed to a place where the land sloped upwards and was covered with boulders. He remembered a place — something from his childhood . . .

Jed Brandt saw their fleeing figures and called his followers from their positions surrounding the building. Willis, unsure of what was happening and fearing an attempt to reach the horses, released the gate of the paddock and sent Jayne's chestnut, the little pack-horse, Milly's elderly mare and the old grey on their way out through the farm gate towards the woods.

Jed Brandt cursed him loud and long for his waste of time, but saw to it that the remainder of the gang went in pursuit of the fugitives. Bullets flew overhead as Nick and Jayne ran like deer up the slope but within a few minutes they had taken shelter in a little hollow amongst the boulders. It was a spot Nick remembered well from his childhood, for it had served as a fort in his games with imaginary foes. Now the enemy was real and more dangerous than a pack of wolves.

Brandt's men took up fresh positions, hiding behind walls and at the corner of outbuildings. Brandt could see that the young feller and the girl were in a position of some advantage, for it was not possible to advance against them without being shot down. It was, however, only temporary. There was no doubt in his mind that prolonged firing with rifles would eventually cut them down, if not by a direct bullet then by ricochet. The rock-face above them slanted in such a way that bullets, fired skilfully, would find a mark. His men knew how to deal with such a situation and he had no doubts as to the eventual outcome.

He was relieved and surprised to find himself faced with no more than a young feller and a girl. He was also angry to think that he had been held back by so weak a force. He was anxious to get on with his real reason for being here, which was to lay his hands on the Mexican silver, not to trade shots with this boy and his little fancy woman. In spite of their obvious youth, they had already proved to be much more than just a walkover. He had two men dead already and Pert was in such a bad way as to be almost useless. He felt strongly that he had to bring matters to a head very soon.

By now it was broad daylight and Brandt studied the slope, trying to figure out a way of shortening the conflict. He could see that the defensive position taken up by Nick had its weaknesses. If a man could climb that slope and remain out of their field of vision it would be possible to work round and approach their hiding-place from overhead. Then two quick bullets would finish the matter there and then.

He gave orders to Willis to keep firing but to make certain that his own safety was not jeopardized as he moved in for the kill. Then he began to walk round and, when he was out of sight, began his long climb. The slope was not too steep and the scattered boulders were a help rather than a hindrance. He began to feel the task would not be so difficult. He should get it over with quite quickly. As he climbed, he glanced down at the house. It seemed to him that the fire was beginning to subside, the wood of the main room having been consumed. He supposed that the kitchen area, from which Rusty's arm still extended, was built mainly of stone.

But there had been a lot of burning.

Thank God old Busby had not brought banknotes back from Mexico! The silver would be safe enough until he could get his hands on it.

In just a few minutes he would begin his gentle climb down behind these two rabbits and blow their brains out.

Down below, Pert was in agony. His shattered leg bled profusely. He had had no help and no sympathy from his comrades and he felt he might die from loss of blood if he did not do something about himself. For that reason, he hauled himself back out of the line of fire and into a ditch that ran by the paddock. There he found a short piece of stick and attempted to make a tourniquet, using his neckerchief. Slowly the cloth tightened and the flow of blood lessened. The pain seemed even worse, however, and he cursed the girl for that shot from the cavalry rifle. How he longed to get his hands on her! He would rip out her throat with his teeth or tear her head off!

There was no chance of that, however, as it was plain that Jed meant to finish them both in his own quick way. Pert lay for some minutes with his face in the dust, seeking to get control of his pain. Then he decided to crawl back to rejoin the fight. Even if one of *his* bullets succeeded in killing the girl, that would be of some satisfaction.

He raised his head and found himself looking beyond the farm buildings. He saw a length of trail and woodland beyond and a big chestnut horse without a saddle standing idly in the morning sun. He spat and began to turn towards the scene of action but then paused and screwed up his eyes.

Over a rise in the trail some horsemen were coming into sight. The man at the head of the little group wore a silver star in his lapel.

8

When Robert Paget rode into Pronghorn Flats the sun had not yet risen and the town lay in the semi-dark of early morning. The buildings were in shadow and there were no lamps to be seen in the windows.

He did not go to the sheriff's office, knowing that Clem Burns would still be fast asleep in his own home but went straight to the sheriff's house, and knocked loudly on the door. Burns was by no means pleased at the rude awakening but listened carefully to what Robert had to say as he pulled on his clothes. 'Shots up at Bluewater? You sure about that?'

'I am. We have to move fast, sheriff. There's no time to be wasted!'

'Am I wasting time, fer Chris'sake? Here, Bob,' he said to the young stable-lad who lodged with him, 'run like fury and rouse up Lamprey and Midge and as many others as you kin find. Tell them it's urgent.'

He wasn't quite certain as to the urgency. It seemed to him that the lawyer, Paget, had been acting a bit queer recently but he could not afford to ignore such information as had just been presented to him. It was his duty to investigate.

After some minutes, Lamprey and Midge arrived, looking sleepy-eyed. They listened to Paget's story and forced themselves properly awake as the sheriff gave out his orders. Shortly afterwards, they were saddling up and preparing to leave.

'You comin' too, Mr Paget?' snapped Burns, noting that Robert had made no move.

'Me? Well . . . '

'It's your nephew up there, ain't it? Anyhow, we ain't goin' to get a big posse together in a couple of minutes. The rest will have to follow as quick as they can make it. Meanwhile, I need anybody I kin get. That means you, Mr Paget. I hereby swear you in as deputy, for today, at any rate.'

He smiled thinly to himself as he led the small cavalcade out of town. He was beginning to dislike Robert Paget. The man had too many strange attitudes, especially about the whole business of Glen Paget's death and Nick's supposed involvement.

They made good time up the trail towards Bluewater but the sun was rising by the time they were within a mile or two of the farm. Burns was in the lead with Lamprey and Midge to either side but a few yards further back. To the rear, Robert rode the black horse. He hung back as far as he dared, ready with the excuse that his horse was tired after its earlier gallop although the truth was that Midnight had too much stamina to be much troubled by the distance he had already travelled that morning.

What happened next was the fault of the sheriff, as his two deputies would have had to admit if they had ever been asked. As the posse got near to the farm it ought to have slowed down altogether and individuals detailed to scout ahead. This morning, Burns, not as alert as he usually was, forgot some of his caution and came over a rise in the trail without realizing how near they were approaching to the farm. He halted when he saw the farm buildings and the smoke blowing away to the south in the morning breeze. For a brief moment, the others stopped too . . .

From his ditch, Pert caught sight of the horsemen at the same moment and saw the silver star shining in the sun. He knew then that he was doomed. Since the law had arrived there was nothing for it but to fight or to run. As there seemed nothing much to fight for, the choice would be to run for it. Brandt and his able-bodied followers would make for their horses and ride like hell to avoid a pointless conflict with the sheriff and his men. They would not stop to help Pert and he knew himself to be too badly hurt to get to a horse or to mount one. That meant being taken into custody to eventually stand under the gallows or to be killed within a short time just where he lay.

The realization came as a bitter shock but he thrust the idea to the back of his mind as the silver star blinked at him. The bitterness was still there but now it transferred itself to the men riding over that rise in the trail. All his life, Pert had hated the law, hated silver stars, hated sheriffs, hated all of it because it had always tried to prevent him from doing what he wanted to do. Now that hatred congealed itself into a loathing that would have destroyed every sheriff in the world if it could have done so.

Pert leaned his elbows quickly over the side of the ditch. He took swift but careful aim with his rifle. It was a long shot but the bullet sped with deadly accuracy. Sheriff Burns jerked upright in the saddle and fell over backwards. He was dead before he struck the ground, his heart ripped by the red-hot lead.

Lamprey and Midge turned quickly to take cover. They seemed to vanish before Pert could lever another cartridge into the breech. There was a man a short distance behind the group who wore a black jacket and rode a black horse. He turned to wheel away and ride back but Pert fired again and he saw the man slump over his mount's neck as it galloped out of sight.

Pert grinned. Even on this, the day of his death, he was having his revenge on some of the bastards who had pursued him through life. He vowed to take a few more with him and stopped for a moment to slip another few shells into his rifle. But he was not to have his wish. Lamprey, the sharpshooter, who, it was claimed, could bring down a squirrel as it leaped from tree to tree, raised his rifle from his place of hiding in the undergrowth and fired once at the far-off head that moved just above the level of the ditch.

The bullet entered the middle of Pert's face and he fell back and died, an inarticulate curse in a blood-filled mouth being the only comment on his existence.

The gang of outlaws was still engaged in trading shots with their opponents on the hillside and did not hear the firing from the outskirts of the farm. It was Jed Brandt from his position on the hill who spotted the sheriff's party as soon as it topped the rise. His reaction was much the same as that of Pert in that he knew at once that all was lost. There was no chance now of stealing the Mexican silver and little enough chance of escaping with his life. He had seen only a very small group of lawmen and he believed two had been shot down by one of his own men — who exactly he did not know — but experience told him that there would be more just over the horizon and there was no time to waste.

He did not hesitate but scrambled back down the hillside, doing his best to keep out of the sights of the Winchester and the carbine, still firing from amid the rocks, and reached the bottom in a small avalanche of stones.

'Bo! Hans! Willis!' he yelled. 'Time to git out of here! It's the law! Git to the horses!'

He ran from the cover of the rocks towards the fence where he had tethered his own horse. It meant running in the open for a few seconds but he felt desperate not to be trapped by the approaching posse and had to accept the chance of being hit by a bullet from the hillside. He heard a lump of lead whistle by but it merely served to increase his speed.

He ran across the open yard where Milly still lay, twisted in death, with her face to the ground. Anger and frustration filled his heart and he spitefully kicked at the corpse as he passed it.

Up in the hillside, Nick saw the action and became blind with rage. Without thinking, he leaped up and began to run down the slope between the large boulders. In his hands he still held the Winchester. Behind him, Jayne shouted at him to stay in cover but he did not hear her, and his anger was such that he could not have obeyed. A moment later and he was running across the same stretch of ground as had Brandt. When he reached Milly's body, he could not help but hesitate. He felt the need to put his hands out to her, to pick her up, to lay her out in a dignified way, but he did none of these things as he was very much aware of the present danger.

He saw Brandt reach a horse and leap into the saddle; at the same time he was aware of other men running in the same direction. He did not know why they ran. He could not guess at their reasons for retreating from a fight where they had the advantage. He knew, also, that he had impulsively given up the protection of the rocks and was now an easy target. The realization came to him as a sudden shock.

His terrible anger was still with him,

however. To see Milly killed had been almost too much to bear. Only the overriding need to get Jayne to a place of relative safety had prevented him from getting to grips with the murderer. Now, to see Milly's corpse kicked as if it were a piece of garbage almost drove him insane with the desperate need for vengeance.

He halted only long enough to train the Winchester on to Brandt's back as the outlaw rode up the opposite slope in his bid to escape the lawmen. Nick pulled the trigger but to no avail. There came only a dull click and he knew Milly had loaded only a few cartridges and these had already been used in the exchange of fire on the hillside.

Two horsemen were well on their way to the near horizon. Two others were now out from the farm and urging their horses in the same direction. There came the boom of a rifle from somewhere on the other side of the farmhouse and one of the outlaws fell heavily to the ground. He got up almost at once and grabbed at his horse's rein but then he stumbled and fell again. The horse ran off and the man rose on to his knees and fired a handgun at Nick, the only target he could see.

The bullet almost killed Nick, grazing the side of his head and dropping him to the ground. Blood poured down his cheek and into his shirt but he got up in time to see the man slump finally into the grass as Lamprey's rifle found its target.

Within a minute or two, the outlaws had vanished over the rising grassland, scattering dairy cattle as they went. Lamprey and Midge rode into sight round the side of the big barn.

'Hey, you all right?' asked Lamprey. 'Looks like you've been hit.'

'Yeah, I'm OK,' answered Nick, still attempting to stem the flow of blood from his head graze. 'Thanks, fellers, you've saved our lives, I reckon.'

'Pigs are gitting away!' shouted Midge in exasperation. 'There's only three of the bastards. Let's go!'

He headed his horse up the opposite slope on the trail of the fleeing gang. Lamprey hesitated only for a moment.

'That guy is goin' to git himself killed today, seems to me. But he's right. We can't let these sinners git away with this! They need to be brought to book.' He was looking at Milly's body, his eyes changing from sorrow to renewed anger. 'To kill a helpless woman is about the worst thing a man kin do! If you and thet girl up there are all right then I'm goin' after them. The law of God demands it!'

He looked searchingly at Nick.

'There'll be more people here soon to look after the lady,' he said quietly. 'See ya! The Lord's vengeance cometh!'

Without another word he spurred his mount into a gallop to follow Midge, who was already almost out of sight.

'Nick!' Jayne called to him as she stumbled down the slope of the hill. 'You've been hit!'

Nick attempted again to stem the blood from his head but his eyes were on Lamprey as the deputy galloped over the rise. He knew he had to follow. There was no way he could let these two gallant men ride into danger without backing them up. It was his fight, anyway. His stepmother lay as a corpse in the dirt.

'Listen, Jayne, I have to go.' He looked at her searchingly. She had turned white and had begun to tremble. It was as if the fear that had been in her throughout the fight had been kept under control but now was beginning to show itself as the danger seemed to recede. 'Do you think you kin hold on until folks come?'

She was staring at Milly's silent, twisted form. Tears appeared in her eyes. Nick took her by the hands and led her round the back of the shed.

'Don't look any more, Jayne. If you can just stay here for a little while, then people will take you back into Pronghorn. Thing is, I really can't let these two deputies ride away after these outlaws. Things could turn bad. They could get the worst of it and we owe them our lives.'

'You could lose yours while you are about it,' she moaned faintly as she sat down at the shed door. 'But there's no help for it. I know what you mean. Give me just a little time and I'll come too . . .'

'No. You've done more than enough. Stay here. You'll be safe. Don't look at Milly any more.'

Nick ran round the corner of the shed, Jayne's carbine already in hand. He did not look back. If he had he would have seen Jayne collapse on the ground, trembling and tearful, all the tension of the past hour overcoming her at last.

There was a horse that he supposed had belonged to one of the raiders standing quietly by the fence. Without hesitation, Nick leaped into the saddle and rode quickly from the farm and up the slopes in the wake of the two deputies. He could make out the tracks of their horses in the grass mixed with those of the gang. He still had no idea who the men were who had attacked the farm and killed Milly but he was certain that he would kill them or die in the attempt. His mind was full of anger as the image of her twisted corpse and the brutal kick it had just taken filled his imagination.

The horse he was riding seemed fresh and he rapidly topped the rise and saw the undulating grassland opening out before him. Far ahead there were riders, three in a group, almost on the horizon and another two widely separated but nearer at hand. The last one, he knew, was Lamprey. He had known the deputy all his life and had listened to his preaching and praying with a mixture of amusement and irritation but now they both shared the same anger.

The three riders well ahead vanished below the horizon but as they went it seemed to Nick that they turned and changed direction towards the south. A glance in that direction brought a glint of blue water to his eye and he guessed they were heading towards the rocky escarpments that ran down to the shore of an arm of the lake. He remembered the area from his boyhood. There were ridges and clefts and little gullies there that provided cover for any man with a rifle. It would make a good place for the outlaws to make a stand if that was their intention. Perhaps they now knew how few were their pursuers. If they could shoot down the two deputies in the open before a larger posse could arrive, they might yet make good their escape.

Nick turned his horse aside, seeking a long line of lower ground that he knew from past experience would lead him towards the rocky escarpments with a chance of cutting off the outlaws before they could set up an ambush. It was an outside chance but it might just work . . .

Nick was right in his surmise as to what was in the mind of Jed Brandt and his men. They were well aware that only two men had followed them up that slope from Bluewater Farm and there was a good chance that they could be gunned down before more arrived. Jed knew about the rocks as he had observed them often enough as he had ridden that way in the past. One thought that was uppermost in his mind was to remain unrecognized. The young guy and the girl on the farm did not know him from Adam but he and Lamprey had met before and Brandt had recognized the sharp-shooter from afar. If the deputy approached much closer he would know without doubt whom he was chasing and there would be no living in peace in the entire territory thereafter.

Lamprey had to die in the very near future — that much was certain.

Brandt, Willis and Bo Hart rode pell-mell to the south, horses panting and beginning to stumble here and there over the rough ground. For the moment the representatives of the law were out of sight but it was clear that horsetracks in the long grass could not be hidden and the change of direction must be seen and followed. By then, however, Brandt intended to be ready.

It was not long before the ground changed to thin clumps of tough grass and scattered stone. Far ahead there stood rocky outcrops. If they could be reached before the gunplay started then Brandt and his men would have cover enough. For the moment they could do nothing but ride.

Their mounts were slobbering and stumbling before they reached the first group of rocks large enough for a man to hide behind.

'Git ready!' yelled Brandt. 'I want one man over there behind thet boulder. The rest where I say. We'll git them two polecats afore they know what day of the week it is.'

'I reckon there's three!' answered Bo. 'I think I seed another feller, way behind.'

'So, we git him too! Hey, Willis, you take the big boulder. Hide your horse down the slope.'

Willis scowled but did not dare defy Brandt. He did not really relish the prospect of being the first in line for the forthcoming action. He leapt to the ground and led his horse down the little slope behind the immense boulder. Then he took up his position, rifle at the ready. A short distance along the ridge, Brandt and Bo prepared themselves in the same way.

It was not long before Midge appeared, riding as if the devil was seated behind him. His rifle was angled across his saddle-bow, his hat blowing back from the string that held it to the back of his neck. He did not hesitate even when he realized that the enemy had disappeared. They were ahead somewhere and it seemed to him there was no time to be lost in coming to grips with them.

The bullet from Willis's rifle took him in the chest and he hit the ground like a sack of corn.

Lamprey heard the report from over the next ridge and guessed immediately what had happened. He cut to one side and made a cautious approach, using what cover he could find amid the few stones that littered the slope. He dismounted because he knew in his heart that Midge had ridden into an ambush. He crawled like a lizard from stone to stone, keeping his head down all the way, until he could see ahead a little. He saw outcrops of granite and huge boulders that seemed to stretch in a long line towards the massive piles of rock that skirted the river as it ran down to Bluewater Lake in the distance.

Not far away stood Midge's horse. A little further on lay Midge himself, on his back in the grass, dead face looking into the sky. Lamprey muttered a prayer for Midge's soul while his mind cursed the polecat who had done the killing. All the while his eyes searched amid the stones. The place seemed quiet. There was no doubt that the rats were lying there in ambush waiting for their next victim.

Then he spotted a hat moving just

beside the huge granite boulder about fifty yards beyond Midge. Lamprey did not hesitate. His long rifle boomed and Willis departed from life without ever knowing what had hit him.

Bullets sang over Lamprey's head but he moved quickly and ran, head down, along the ridge towards better cover. It was then that his luck ran out. A stone moved from under his boot and he fell, twisting his ankle. As he rolled, he felt a pain like a bayonet thrusting into his stomach as one of Bo's slugs found its mark, and he believed then that he was a dead man.

Brandt and Bo saw him fall and jerk as the bullet struck him and yelled together in triumph. They ran out from the cover of the boulders, rifles in hand, ready to finish him off and get on their way. They halted momentarily as they saw his expression of contempt.

'I thought it was you, Brandt. I see the devil in your eyes, and Old Nick standin' at your elbow, ready to welcome you to hell!'

9

Nick heard the shots as he urged his mount up the slope towards the top of the ridge. Already he could see outcrops of rock but he knew none of the riders ahead had yet reached the massive granite slabs near the river. He had failed to find a spot from which to lie in wait and the sudden outbreak of gunfire meant that he could hesitate no longer. As he topped the rise he saw two raiders, one a bearded man, run over the stony ground to a figure lying in the grass.

Nick guessed at once that Lamprey lay there and that he was wounded. Within a second or two he would die under the guns of his executioners. Nick lifted the carbine and fired as soon as he steadied the horse.

The slug sang past Brandt's ear and he fell instinctively to one knee. Bo did likewise but in a moment they recovered from their surprise sufficiently to crouch in what cover was available and return fire. Nick urged his horse into a gallop and reached a large boulder as the bullets went over his head. He jumped from the saddle and slid a little way down the slope where his outstretched feet accidentally kicked the twisted corpse of Willis and sent it a few inches further downhill.

He wasted no time in clambering to a better position from which he had a view of the place where he had last seen the two men as they stood over their victim. He could see the crown of a black hat half hidden by a stone and, a few yards to the right, the muzzle of a rifle protruding from a clump of long grass. Nick sighed, momentarily relieved that their attention was withdrawn from Lamprey.

He fired the carbine again and the hat vanished. A second later and two rifles fired simultaneously, chipping fragments of granite from his protecting boulder. He took aim again at once but could see no sign of a target. He knew they had spread out, keeping low, and searching for better vantage points. In a very short time, he would be under fire from both sides.

He could not afford to wait for that. They would kill him for sure. He had seen the black hat over to the right and he was certain that it was the guy with the black beard who had been wearing it. It was the same brutal rat who had attempted to shoot Jayne and himself from behind on the farm hillside and who had enraged him by kicking Milly's body in the yard. It seemed to Nick that if he could only take one man with him then it must be that particular hell-hound.

He left the shadow of the rock and crept along the ridge, hoping to catch a glimpse of the enemy before he was spotted himself. He kept very close to the ground and moved as silently as possible. He peered from behind a rugged piece of granite, hoping that he had not been observed, but could see no sign of life. All was silent save the rushing of wind through the grass and the idle movement of horses some distance away.

He felt at a loss as to what to do to bring his enemies out into the open. They were hidden somewhere amid the scattering of rocks over the ridge but he reckoned they were too smart to give up the cover they had. It was a waiting game with death the likely punishment for a break in concentration or a moment of impatience. What made it harder to bear was the knowledge that Lamprey lay somewhere on the other slope with a bullet in him with no prospect of help. On the other hand, these outlaws could not afford to hang around too long, knowing that more lawmen might be on their way.

The stalemate was broken at last by a slight movement away over to the left, further off than Nick had expected. There was a hint of blue moving just beside a boulder. Nick racked his brain trying to remember whether Lamprey had worn a blue checked shirt, as it occurred to him that the wounded man might be attempting to crawl away in that direction. Then he remembered Lamprey's jacket of rawhide and decided it was safe to fire. He took rapid aim just as the blue changed to black and pulled the trigger. There came a yell of agony and Bo Hart leaped momentarily into view, clutching his left leg. Then the man was gone, desperate to return to cover.

It was then that everything went against Nick. It seemed that a hammer blow was dealt to the carbine as a slug from Brandt's rifle struck the barrel and ricocheted off, missing Nick's face by a hair's breadth. He knew in an instant that his finger was broken and his arm seemed turned to stone so that the weapon fell from his grasp.

Brandt rose in an instant from behind a rock and came bounding over the intervening space. His face was distorted in a mixture of wild fury and triumph. He fired his rifle again as he came but excitement interfered with his aim and the bullet went wide.

Nevertheless, Nick had no opportunity to defend himself. His numbed hand would not grip the Colt in his holster. In a moment, Brandt hovered over him, gun pointing, ready to deal out death.

'Kill the bastard!' yelled Bo, running and limping through the grass.

Brandt hesitated. He recognized Nick as the young guy from the farm, his intended victim, and the one person Robert Paget had wanted to be rid of more than any other. His eyes bored into Nick's face while his lips sought to form a question. It seemed to him that all of this goddamned raid had turned out to be nothing but a dangerous fiasco and it was hard to ride away from it with nothing at all but the lawyer's money. Was it possible that this young feller might know something about his grandfather's silver hoard? There was time for a quick question and there was no harm in asking.

'Listen, polecat,' he hissed, anger seething, in his voice. 'Your only chance of staying alive is to tell me about old man Busby's Mexican silver. Where is it? Tell me and you won't git your brains blown out. Don't take no time to think about it because ya don't have any . . . '

Nick's head wound had reopened and the blood poured down his face. It had gone into one eye and his surprised expression was not too obvious. He, like everyone else, had heard of the silver but had been told nothing of it by his father. All his young life he had believed that old Busby had spent it himself. He had seldom thought about it over the years. Now he knew what this savage raid had been about and he saw, in his imagination, his uncle Robert's sly face and knew for certain why he had wanted rid of Milly and himself.

Brandt's finger whitened on the trigger.

'All right.' Nick's tone was one of

resignation, deliberately assumed to disguise the sense of relief that came to him. He realized that he could live a little longer and, like all men under the threat of a gun, he found that he valued every minute granted to him. 'I'll tell you but you need to promise me that I'll go free.'

It was a lie and the answer — as he knew — was a lie also.

'Sure, you'll be as free as a bird!' answered Brandt, thinking of a chicken with its neck wrung. 'But be quick as hell about it!'

Nick thought quickly. It came into his head to say the stuff was at the farm but he knew Brandt would not venture back there with the threat of the law waiting for him. It had to be somewhere where Brandt thought he stood a chance of finding it without delay. There was not much time. Bo Hart was cursing and rubbing his leg and staring anxiously back at the way they had come.

'The silver is under a stone, way over

there, near Indian Rock.'

'Indian Rock?' Brandt turned his head to look in the direction of the river. He had heard of the strange, twisted hunk of granite that was supposed to look like an Indian from a certain angle although he had never troubled to look carefully at it. Nick had. He had made a few sketches of it in his youth, drawing the rugged profile of long nose and stubborn chin with the sun behind, emphasizing its shape.

'It's there.' Nick spoke calmly, keeping the pain of his hand out of his face and voice. 'My old man and Feather Dan hid it there years ago . . . ' Why, he wondered, had he mentioned Feather Dan? Something was wriggling about in the depths of his mind but he had no time to sort it out. He had to persuade Brandt, to lead him somewhere, to change this situation, to create an opportunity, however slight, of turning the tables. 'I know exactly where it is. But you need to let me go free, and the deputy too.'

'The goddamned deputy? All right. Lead me to it. I git a feeling you're lying but you kin have as long as it takes to reach them rocks — after thet time runs out fer all of us, especially you!'

Bo stood guard, one hand on his bleeding leg, while Brandt relieved Nick of his guns and then brought in the horses. He left Willis's horse grazing some distance away. It was evident to Nick that he was not thinking of an extra pack-horse to carry the silver. In Brandt's mind, there was no need. There would be two extra horses anyway.

Lamprey was found, kneeling in the grass, hands clasped to his bleeding side. He said nothing but nodded when Brandt told him to mount. He did so with help from Nick and a good shove from Bo. He hung forward in his pain as they rode. Bo and Brandt took up the rear, guns trained on their prisoners.

As they neared the rocky escarpment, Nick's anxiety rose. Every yard brought the moment of truth nearer. In a very few minutes he would have to take action. Brandt had no time to lose. His patience was already running out fast and the gun trained on Nick's back might be fired at any moment. He was obviously not convinced by Nick's story and it would take only another hesitation or faintly suspicious move or delay to set his Colt blazing.

Indian Rock loomed just ahead, the rugged profile dark against the bright light of the sun. Brandt glanced up at it with no curiosity. There was nothing in his mind but the business in hand and the danger that might well be growing on the trail behind them.

'Git movin', Paget,' he growled. 'You got a couple of minutes to show me you're telling the truth, thet's all we have time for.'

The grass thinned out and was replaced by scattered stone and rock. Soon they were riding through stands of granite, grey and split by centuries of sun and rain. Beyond, the land dropped away to the river — still unseen

— which eventually flowed into Bluewater Lake. Lamprey was swaying in the saddle, his face almost on a level with his horse's neck. Blood seeped through his shirt and over his leg. He seemed on the point of collapse but had looked up under beetled brows at Brandt's words. It was as if it was not until this moment that he had realized why they had ridden this way.

'This is all hokum!' snarled Bo Hart. 'Let's git rid of thet lying skunk and git out of here!'

'Shaddap!' snapped Brandt but his finger tightened on the trigger. 'Now, Paget, we're at the end of your trail . . . '

There was no time left. Nick knew Brandt had come to the limit of his patience. He held up a hand as if he had suddenly discovered the spot he had been looking for.

'This is it,' he said. 'Under that stone.'

'Git down and move it,' snapped Brandt, with no conviction in his voice.

Nick slid to the ground. The stone he had pointed out was of dark, heavy granite. There was no doubt in his mind that it had remained undisturbed in the soil for centuries. He looked up at Brandt, his mind jumping like a grasshopper.

'I can't shift it on my own. It will take two anyway and I can't grip with this bad hand. That last bullet of yours did a lot of damage.'

'Pity it didn't take out your goddamned brains!' yelled Bo, the pain in his leg reaching fever pitch. 'Git on with it or I'll fix you good, myself! Move, fer Chris'sake!'

Lamprey, lurching in the saddle a couple of yards away, straightened himself up a little and stared. His eyes — already filled with the mist of coming death — showed pin-points of anger.

'Give the useless bastard a hand,' ordered Brandt.

'I can't goddamned well stand,' objected Bo. 'This leg is like hell.'

Cursing, Brandt jumped from the saddle, while motioning to Bo to keep his gun trained. He glanced at the boulder and then looked hard at Nick.

'If you're lying you won't git your brains blown out but I'll carve out your belly with all the bullets in this here gun!'

He replaced his Colt in its holster, knowing Bo was still on guard, and bent down to grip the edge of the stone. Nick bent his knees as if to put all his strength into raising the stone and stretched out his hands to its rough surface. He knew he had come to the final moment of his pretence. Now, he must launch himself at Brandt and hope to overcome him. It was a desperate idea. Brandt was a big and powerful man and Nick's right arm was almost useless. Also, Bo's gun did not waver for an instant.

Then Brandt stood up once again. It was as if he had seen something through a space in the rocks behind Nick. His eyes narrowed as if he looked into the distance. His hand touched again the butt of his handgun. Bo glanced in the same direction. Far off, in the grassland, two tiny figures could be seen riding from the east, perhaps coming for Indian Rock, but more likely heading for Bluewater Farm.

'Christ in Hell!' Bo shouted. 'Riders comin'!'

That blasphemy was too much for Lamprey. He stuck his heels into his mount and sent it bounding forward into the rear of Bo's horse. At the same time, he threw himself at the outlaw, gripping his shirt in both hands. Both men tumbled to the ground with a thud.

Brandt whirled, gun already drawn, but he did not fire. Nick guessed why. Brandt had no wish to attract the attention of the far-off riders with gunshots. If the men intended coming to this rocky place for some reason, then it would have to be settled by gunplay, but if they rode by, all unawares, then so much the better.

Nick launched himself at Brandt's legs. The big man toppled but swung round and struck out with his pistol at Nick's head. Blood sprang anew through the fair hair but Nick changed his grip and managed to reach the Colt with his left hand. He held on grimly while Brandt lashed out with his fist, striking him on the side of the face. Then Brandt gripped Nick round the neck and they rolled through the loose stones, each trying to master the other. Nick knew he was getting the worst of it but used his legs to good effect, constantly pushing and kicking with his feet in an effort to stay on top. Once under Brandt's weight and he would have no chance.

Brandt twisted his arm and pointed the Colt at Nick's head at point-blank range. He had got past worrying about the strangers. His anger was such that he would have taken on an entire posse if it had appeared. Desperately, Nick held on to the strong wrist and turned the barrel of the gun to the air. In a moment, however, he knew he would be finished. His strength was running out. Then he felt his feet slip from under him and he guessed that their struggle had brought them to the steep bank leading to the edge of the river. He held on to Brandt and threw all his weight downwards.

They rolled down the slope with increasing speed. An avalanche of small stones went with them. Then the ground seemed to drop away and they hit the water and went under in a second. Nick had instinctively filled his lungs with air as he had felt himself falling. The river was about six feet deep at this point where it swirled around the foot of the little rocky bluff and both men were still locked in combat. It came into Nick's mind that death was very near.

He twisted round and gained a grip with his left arm round the neck of his opponent. The fact that they were both in the river lessened the advantage that Brandt had had a few seconds ago on the bank. His extra weight and strength were cancelled out by their weightlessness under water. Nick tightened his grip, squeezing his arm round the thick neck as tightly as he could.

Their feet hit the stones of the riverbed. Brandt kicked out and put a hand behind his own head to grasp Nick's right ear. They struggled like wild animals, then Brandt kicked downwards again and they reached the surface, drawing in air in fierce gasps. Nick lost his grip and saw Brandt's face turn towards him, a mask of wet fury. Strong hands gripped Nick by the collar of his shirt and forced him under. He struggled to no avail and felt himself to be drowning. He knew he could not hold his breath a moment longer. His left hand — the only one he had much control over — came up and the fingers sought out Brandt's eyes. More by luck than good judgement he found his index finger in an eye socket and thrust home with all his might. The grip on his shirt loosened and he pulled free and shot to the surface.

Brandt had found his footing on the shelving riverbed and was struggling ashore. There was blood in his eye. He too was gasping for breath. He bent down to pick up a heavy stone and swung it at Nick's head. The blow almost knocked Nick off his feet but he threw himself towards the bank in time to prevent himself from falling once again into the water — this time, undoubtedly to drown — and fell to his knees on the wet shingle.

Brandt was upon him within seconds with murder in his one open eye and a knife in his hand. Desperately, Nick rose, grabbed at the knife arm and held it back for a moment, although he knew his strength was not equal to that of Brandt. They swayed violently, feet slipping from under them on the bank . . .

Then Nick glanced past his opponent's bulky form and noted with a little surprise that they had been carried only a couple of hundred yards downstream and the rocky escarpment still loomed against the sky. The fact hardly registered, such was his state of mind, but his eyes picked out a movement in that brief second and he saw the glitter of a rifle barrel on top of the slope of the bank beneath the rocks and recognized the head of Bo Hart behind it.

The rifle was aimed at himself. That piece of knowledge was in his mind as soon as he saw the gun and in the brief moment of time in which he struggled to hold back Brandt's knife. Almost instinctively, he pulled hard at the bigger man's arm, and threw his weight to one side. Brandt swung round, feet slipping on the stones, and then gasped as the bullet took him in the back.

Nick fell to the ground. He glanced up and saw Brandt lurch to one side and fall headlong into the river. He came up once, mouth open, seeming to call for help, but no word came to his lips. Then he was gone with the current.

Nick could not move. He felt numb.

His body seemed to have been frozen in a pit of ice. Only his heart and lungs hammered in an attempt to cling on to life. He felt as if he were about to die. The pebbles and wet silt beneath his chest and arms and legs seemed to drag him down to an early grave.

It was the thought of Lamprey that somehow brought him back to an awareness of his surroundings and his own acute danger. He had last seen the badly wounded deputy as he sprang at Bo Hart and grabbed at his clothing. It seemed, however, that Bo had survived which meant that Lamprey was dead.

The notion brought fresh anger into Nick's mind and stimulated him into making an attempt to rise. He stared upstream towards the stands of granite but could not focus his eyes. He wiped water from them with his one good hand and made out their gaunt shapes standing like grotesque statues against the light.

He also saw the gleam of the rifle. The weapon moved briefly and then pointed steadily in his direction. Bo Hart was prepared to fire again. No doubt the shock of having killed his own leader had made him hesitate for a few minutes but now he was readying himself for the shot that would bring vengeance upon the skunk who had brought such disaster upon the gang of raiders and turned easy success into dismal failure.

Nick looked about him. There was nowhere to run to even if he had been able to move with any speed. He was trapped in the open and already caught in the sights of Bo's rifle and he knew the killing mind behind it would show no mercy.

10

The rifle remained trained upon him and he knew that in a matter of seconds his heart or brain could be torn out by a red-hot bullet. There was silence but for the surge of river-water nearby. It came into his mind that if he could reach the river he might give himself a chance by throwing himself into the current and vanishing from sight. Very probably he would drown but it might be better than the certainty of a bullet.

He turned his head towards the rushing water. It was at some yards distance but he took a tentative step in that direction and then jumped in shock as he heard the boom of the rifle and heard the bullet sing overhead. His foot slipped on wet stone and he fell, his injured head striking on a bed of pebbles. He felt the mists of unconsciousness close over him, smothering his surprise in the knowledge that the shot had been so wide off the target . . .

When he slowly regained his senses, he knew by the position of the sun in his eyes that a long time had passed. He lay on his back in water and tried to reassemble his thoughts, before rising stiffly and standing, half-crouched, to stare towards the rocks from which the shot had come.

Slowly his eyes focused and he made out the shape of the gunman's head at the top of the steep slope with the shadow of the overhanging granite behind it. There was no hint of life and no movement, just the stillness of death.

Nick stepped cautiously forward, staring at the still figure. Nothing could be seen but the top of the man's head and one outstretched arm hanging over the edge of rock. As he approached he saw that the rifle was jammed in a little crevasse half way down the steep slope as if it had slipped from Bo Hart's grasp.

A little further on, he came to a point where the bank was gentler and he could make his way up with greater ease. His climb to the top was hard going, nevertheless, as he could use only one hand and his head throbbed with every movement. He lay panting for a moment and stared around. The corpse of his enemy was lying face down with outstretched legs. The blue-checked shirt was heavily blood-stained and there was a pool of drying blood under the man's leg.

Nick got to his feet and stepped cautiously over the short intervening distance. The dead face was half-buried in the dirt but what could be seen of it was twisted in agony. There was a deep, gaping wound through the back of the shirt and a few yards away lay a large bone-handled knife. Nick had seen the weapon at the belt of the man who now lay dead on the stones before him. It seemed evident that he had been stabbed by his own knife and had pulled it from his back before crawling to the edge of the rocks to take revenge on his last remaining enemy.

A short distance further on, near the stone which was supposed to have hidden the silver, lay Lamprey, dead eyes staring into the sky with just a hint of a smile at the corners of his mouth.

Nick stood still for some minutes, feeling quite unable to move. He had never been a close friend of Lamprey but had respected him for a man who was steadfast in his principles. He was a good deputy, intent upon doing his duty. Also, it had seemed to Nick that they had shared a common goal in seeking to destroy the band of raiders who had killed Milly. The memory of Milly lying crumpled in the dirt saddened him and still filled him with anger. Now, however, there was no one left to turn his anger upon — except Robert Paget. He it was who was behind all the killing and the terrible tragedy. Nick's hand felt for his side-gun but realized that it was not there. Brandt had taken it and thrown it somewhere amongst the stones. At the thought, Nick turned from the dead deputy and searched for the Colt but with no success. Brandt had disposed of it some distance away. At length he decided to take Hart's gun which was still in its holster. He felt like a thief as he withdrew it, for robbing the dead was not in his nature, but it seemed to him that he might yet have need of such a weapon.

He went back to the place where the deputy lay and covered the dead face with a hat that he found nearby. It seemed to him that there was now an air of finality about everything. The fight was over. By good fortune, he had survived. He felt a natural relief in the knowledge that there was no more danger at present and with that thought turned his attention to the need to return to Bluewater.

Bo Hart's horse was standing some yards away and Nick realized the necessity of bringing it in hand. The other horses had wandered down from the ridge and were feeding on the rough grass in the distance.

He caught the animal without difficulty but grunted in pain as he mounted up. His head throbbed and his arm hurt badly as he put strain upon it but he turned towards home, swaying in the saddle, and with his head pounding the harder with every movement.

He had gone only a couple of miles when he met up with a group of men from Pronghorn all armed with rifles. They carried their guns across their saddle-bows as if ready for instant action. He knew by the look of them that they were not regular lawmen but a posse gathered together in haste and with little appetite for the job. Only one wore the badge of a deputy. Nick recognized him as Tim Hewitt, who worked at the livery stables in Pronghorn.

Several of these men raised their rifles when they saw Nick but lowered them when Tim raised a friendly hand in greeting.

'Hey, Nick Paget! What the hell, you

look as if you've been mixing it with them bandits! We're out to git them. Thing is, though, we've been held up what with the sheriff being killed an' all . . . ' His voice trailed off for a moment, then he said: 'You know where these guys are?'

'Up at Indian Rock — what's left of them,' grunted Nick. He found it difficult to talk. His mouth seemed stiff. When he put his hand up to his head he noted with surprise that his hair was matted in dried blood. 'You'll find a couple of your deputies too, I'm sorry to say. Good brave fellers they were too — only they ran into an ambush. You won't need your guns. Whole thing is over with.'

He felt faint but steadied himself by clinging harder to the pommel of the saddle.

'You all right, Mr Paget?' There was a hint of relief in the man's tone as he realized that there was no need for a showdown with the raiders. 'Need any help?'

Nick shook his head and said no more. He continued at a slow pace while the posse rode away at increased speed in the direction of Indian Rock.

He was within a mile of Bluewater when he made out three riders coming towards him. At first he did not recognize them at all, then he sat up in surprise as he made out Jayne and her two brothers. They halted as he approached and stared at him in silence before Flint, the elder of the two brothers, spoke.

'Nick Paget, ain't it? We've been hearing all about you. Jayne's been telling us. You look pretty bad. Kin we help?'

'It's all right,' answered Nick, still struggling to speak. He was looking at Jayne. She sat astride the same chestnut horse she had ridden into Bluewater a couple of days earlier but she was still wearing her nightdress under one of her brothers' coats. She looked tired and strained but smiled at him, relief showing in her face.

'You all right, Jayne?' he asked anxiously.

'She's surviving,' cut in John, as if to save her the trouble of answering. 'Thing is, we heard from this kid, by the name of Jasper, thet there was trouble over at Pronghorn and Bluewater, so we rode over fast as we could. We knew Jayne intended visiting . . . visiting Milly. Say, we're real sorry about what happened to Milly! We knew Jayne had taken Milly's old picture so we guessed she would be at Bluewater. Then, half-ways over, we heard a couple of shots from somewhere. Thet really scared us, I kin tell you!'

'Me too,' grunted Nick ruefully.

'We're taking our little sister home now,' said Flint. 'She needs looking after.'

'Don't get too protective,' put in Jayne with some irritation. 'I'm not a child!'

'You look after her good,' said Nick warmly. 'She's a real heroine, I can tell you!' He caught her eye, which held a hint of tenderness, and his heart leapt. 'Maybe I can come over to visit in a day or two.'

'You'll be welcome,' said John.

'I'll make the decisions!' interrupted Jayne. 'What Nick means is that he wants to visit me, not you two! You'll be more than welcome, Nick, believe me!'

Her eyes told him what he wanted to know and his spirits rose still further when she urged her horse forward and held out her hand to him. He took it and felt the pressure of her fingers.

'What are you going to do now, Nick?' she asked. 'You need to get these injuries seen to!'

'I'll see the doctor in Pronghorn but first . . . ' He hesitated as he realized for the first time how the situation had changed. 'I want to have a look at my place to see what's left of it!'

'Men from the town have been there, Nick. They took Milly away.' Jayne's voice was soft and sympathetic. 'That's for the best at any rate. You make sure you come over to our place, Nick.'

'I want to,' he answered fervently. He meant to say more but now was not the time. 'I'll see you in a couple of days.'

'See the doctor today, Nick,' she advised, 'then come as soon as you can.'

They rode away but Flint shouted back: 'Them bandits . . . where did they get to?'

'Feller called Lamprey reckoned they had all gone to hell!' called out Nick. 'Could be he was right — anyhow, you won't be seeing them.'

'Jest missed the polecats!' growled John to himself.

When Nick arrived at the farm he hitched Bo's horse to the fence and then walked warily towards the house, troubled at what he might see. It was an immense relief that Milly's body had been carried away to the undertaker's. The other corpses had gone too and there was little but spent cartridges to tell that a gunfight had taken place.

The house was in ruins. The two main rooms had been gutted by the fire and still smouldered. The kitchen, being built mainly of stone, had survived although the sink was still heavily bloodstained. He turned away from it in some disgust but then stepped through the wide opening that had been the window of the parlour and made his way over the ashes. Glass from the windows — a luxury Glen Paget had been particularly proud of — crackled beneath his heels. The furniture was burnt black and hardly recognizable. The carpet had been reduced to dust with only a few fragments remaining.

He glanced around in despair as he thought how much had to be done to repair the terrible damage. So this was the place he was inheriting on the death of his stepmother! Well, he would work until it was put to rights, he was determined on that!

As he glanced at the floor a glint of metal caught his eye. He bent down and touched a brass ring in the singed floorboard. He pulled at it with his pain-free hand and, to his surprise, drew up a trap-door of about a couple of feet square. Under it was a hole dug into the earth with stones supporting the sides. He saw nothing but dirt and a scrap of sackcloth and was about to let the trap fall again when a small round shape gleamed faintly in the dim light.

He knew at once it was a coin and lay down awkwardly on the floor to stretch in with his left arm. He caught the rounded edge and pulled it out of the earth and stood up and rubbed the dirt from it on his jacket.

It was a coin, as he had thought, silver, with a value of eight *reales*, and with words in Spanish inscribed upon it. On one side was the figure of a past president of Mexico and on the other, an ancient symbol of the Aztec Indians, long since adopted by the Mexican government as a suitable design for their coinage. The engraving was of an eagle perched upon a cactus and with a struggling snake in its bill and talons.

Then it came to him. He heard again Milly's voice, shrill and mad, as she boasted of dumping all the ornaments and much of the furniture into the Bluewater Lake . . . the bronze bust, the willow pattern plates, the eagles and snakes!

Eagles and snakes. Of course, a common enough name for Mexican coins with their distinctive design!

So that was where old Busby's loot had eventually ended up — in the deepest part of the lake where Milly had deliberately disposed of it with the help of the mule cart and Feather Dan.

Glen must have known about the money. No doubt he had spent some of it and had been planning to use the rest but she had taken her revenge on him for his bullying and jealousy. In the end both had paid the penalty in fear and suffering. Then, guessed Nick, Robert Paget had stepped in to get what he could out of the situation and had preyed upon Milly's terror of the gallows. He had not, however, discovered the whereabouts of the silver. If he had, he would not have instigated the gunfight and slaughter that had just occurred.

So it seemed to Nick as he stood for a long time, gazing at the coin in his hand. Then he slipped the eight *reales* into a pocket, making up his mind to keep it as a souvenir.

Anyway, he had fallen heir to Bluewater and would gradually build it up and make it worthwhile. He would do it for himself and for Jayne. He knew it must be for them both — her eyes and her voice had told him that — and with such knowledge in his heart, he could not fail.

For a moment the image of uncle Robert came into his mind and his hand gripped the butt of Bo Hart's handgun. Then he released the weapon and let it slide back into his holster. There had been plenty of violence and more would do nothing but bring somebody to the gallows — probably himself. Some day, Robert would slip out of the picture, all alone, with nobody to help him do it. Life was like a picture. It was the first time Nick had ever thought of it like that — it was all colour and form until you got to the edges and then nothing but a blank rim . . . unless Lamprey was right and you went out with guns blazing and offering your apologies as you went for disturbing the peace on the other side of the canvas . . .

Suddenly, Nick thought about Bluecoat Ridge. When old man Robert died, he, Nick, would be next in line for that farm too. Robert was too mean and too lonely to make a will for the benefit of anyone. The realization made Nick whistle and he was still whistling when he walked over to Bo Hart's horse and pulled himself painfully into the saddle.

About a couple of miles from Pronghorn, but well off the beaten track, Robert Paget slowly regained consciousness. He knew he had been lying in the grass for a long time, ever since he had lost his grip on the reins of the black horse and had fallen heavily to the ground. He was on his back and he knew he was dying. The slug he had taken from one of his erstwhile allies was lodged somewhere deep within him and he could feel blood gurgling wildly through his body and flowing freely to the ground beneath.

He felt very bad. Black midnight smothered his mind only to withdraw for a moment before returning. He knew it would soon blot him out completely as if the sun had fallen below the dark horizon, never to rise again. The idea scared him but he was too weak to attempt to rise or to help himself in any way. As his eyes focused for a moment he saw only grass and a few milk cows nearby and he knew he was all alone in the world.

When he fought back into consciousness for the final time, however, it was to see an old grey horse with a drooping head standing by. It had sad eyes and, as it gazed at him, the eyes seem to turn even sadder as if they looked into his soul and were saddened beyond measure by what they saw there.